ALSO BY RACHEL CLINE

What to Keep

MY LIAR

RANDOM HOUSE | NEW YORK

My Liar *A Novel*

RACHEL CLINE

Copyright © 2008 by Rachel Cline

Published in the United States by Random House,
an imprint of The Random House Publishing Group,
a division of Random House, Inc., New York.

RANDOM HOUSE and colophon are registered
trademarks of Random House, Inc.

LIBRARY OF CONGRESS CATALOGING-IN-PUBLICATION DATA
Cline, Rachel.
My liar : a novel / Rachel Cline.
p.   cm.
ISBN 978-1-4000-6227-0
1. Women motion picture editors—Fiction.   2. Women motion
picture producers and directors—Fiction.   3. Female friendship—
Fiction.   4. Motion picture industry—Fiction.   5. Power (Social
sciences)—Fiction.   6. Domestic fiction.   I. Title.
PS3603.L555M9 2008
813'.6—dc22   2007019601

Printed in the United States of America on acid-free paper

www.atrandom.com

9 8 7 6 5 4 3 2 1

FIRST EDITION

Book design by Dana Leigh Blanchette

For J.G.

"I am quite happy in a movie, even a bad movie. Other people, so I have read, treasure memorable moments in their lives."

—Walker Percy, *The Moviegoer*

For many who attended, David Bronstein's memorial service was their first experience of mourning a friend. They were dazed by the enormity and absurdity of it. David, after all, had been smart and funny and healthy, well known and well liked—one of them. He had also blown open his head in the balcony of the old Fox Westwood Village. No one had witnessed the act itself, but for those who had to clean up at the theater and particularly for David's friend Josh, who was called to identify the body and drive home David's sad, empty Aries, the aftermath had been gruesome enough.

The service was held while the jacaranda blossoms were out. A common joke about L.A. is that it has three seasons: mud, fire, and earthquakes. But mockers rarely mention the few weeks each spring when a violet haze transforms the city's flat, white daylight as completely and freakishly as inhaled helium changes a familiar voice. As the mourners found their way to the service that after- noon, the jacaranda display took on added meanings: the tawdri- ness and ephemerality of life in the entertainment business, of course, but also the sweetness of that life when everything seemed to be going right, as it sometimes did and, hopefully, would again before too long.

The mourners met at the University Synagogue on Sunset Boulevard. David's parents had once hoped he would be bar mitz- vahed there, but at twelve he had dropped out of Hebrew school, already squirming away from their expectations. The chapel had seating in the round, like that of a Quaker meetinghouse, and the afternoon light streamed in through the clerestory windows. It felt peaceful and safe, or should have.

As Annabeth Jensen looked around at the faces of her ex- boyfriend's mourners, she saw levels of distress that went beyond ordinary sadness. A woman she couldn't identify had been weep- ing openly since taking her seat across from Annabeth. Her face was already red and wrinkled like an enraged infant's. On the aisle at Annabeth's left sat one of the extraordinarily groovy counter workers from Vidiots, the store where she and David used to rent movies. She didn't know his name—David might have—but he was jarringly handsome, with Cherokee cheek- bones, tribal tattoos on his biceps, and silver rings on his thumbs and middle fingers. He was covering his mouth and shuddering with vehement sorrow.

Annabeth felt like a dry-eyed scoundrel. Since first learning of David's death three weeks earlier, she'd been driving around Los

Angeles trying to find her sadness in the landscape, but every landmark had seemed to remind her, instead, of something about David that she'd hated. At the intersection of Pico and Cloverfield, she'd remembered his constant need to debate which farmers' market vendor had the best apples; waiting for her turn to merge onto the 10 from Lincoln Boulevard, she'd flashed on the way his smile revealed far too much of his upper gum; even driving past the Brentwood Country Mart on the way to the service that day, she'd found herself remembering his hideous blue Flojos— the special flip-flops he drove to Tijuana to replace every other year. And that, in turn, reminded her of the three months he'd spent limping after cutting his foot on the morning of the Northridge earthquake—his wounded quality was so much a part of his persona at that point that she'd almost forgotten the original injury. The earthquake seemed like another lifetime. She half-remembered the Nirvana song he'd been singing while they lay in bed that morning, how creepy he'd sounded. She probably should have seen that he was losing it then, but as she'd listened to the dogs barking and the transformers imploding and their world seemingly falling apart, David's darkness hadn't seemed that different from her own. She still couldn't really believe he'd done it—and with a gun. No room for mistakes there. But letting down his listeners, betraying the abject, bottomless love of his parents? That wasn't the David she thought she'd known. She stole a look at Naomi Bronstein, in the front row. David's mother was the daughter of Holocaust victims. Her brimming blue eyes were trained on her lap, but Annabeth could see the fierce effort it cost her just to sit there, to sit still.

David's uncle—not the lawyer but the burnout from Mendocino—had begun speaking his piece. Uncle Ralph had been David's de facto older brother, the one who introduced pudgy, adolescent David to marijuana smoke and the late, psychedelic sound of the Temptations. "With headphones on, and a little reefer in our hearts, we're all black folks," he said to the congregation of mourners, which did include a few genuinely black people: a friend from the Frisbee team at Vassar; coworkers from the Beverly Hills Public Library; and Eunice, the Bronstein's former housekeeper. Annabeth saw Eunice shaking her head slowly from side to side. It was impossible to tell whether she was expressing sorrow or disbelief.

The next speaker was David's friend and next-door neighbor, Josh—the one who'd been home when the LAPD showed up that day. Josh shook back his shoulder-length brown hair and blinked himself into composure after a millisecond of emotional fog. "David's disembodied voice was in some ways all of our best friend," he said. Despite his peculiar grammar, Josh had a point. Many near-strangers had come to the service. They were there to mourn the loss of David's diffident, earnest voice on the radio, talking them home during the city's most solitary and contemplative hours, midnight to three A.M. Tuesdays and Thursdays. Thinking of the times she had heard her boyfriend's voice on the radio late at night, the times he seemed to have read her mind with his choice of music, Annabeth realized she was rocking gently. The stranger beside her, a gray-haired woman who might have been an old elementary school teacher of David's, gestured vaguely, indicating her half-saturated tissue: she had others, but Annabeth shook her head.

David's father, Jerry, the last to speak, looked awful. "Naomi and I are grateful to you for coming, and I know David would have been glad to see you all here," he said, but he broke off there, eventually folding up the paper from which he had apparently expected to read. When he regained his composure, he asked for a few minutes of silent meditation and returned to his seat. What had stopped him was the sight of David's high school girlfriend looking back at him. He couldn't remember her name. Bonnie? She'd been the one to call them that other time, from the emergency room, when David had thrust his hand through a friend's shower door. No one had then mentioned suicide, or even depression—the cure had been stitches and the cancellation of David's planned summer trip to work in an Alaskan cannery, which Jerry had never liked the sound of, anyway. But when he saw the uncomfortable resignation in the girl's now-adult and angular face, the dime had dropped. She was sad but not surprised.

Annabeth had never spent much time with Naomi and Jerry—she sensed that they disapproved of her, mostly because of her Scandinavian Lutheran heritage, although she never said as much to David and he would never have mentioned such a thing to her, even if it was true. But now she was certain that they blamed her. Even though her separation from David was supposedly mutual and they'd parted as friends, the whole thing was far too recent. She'd even talked to him on the phone a few days before his death. His parents probably knew that, too. But although he'd been full of complaints that day (KCRW's new music director's taste was soulless and empty, the Santa Monica Bay was full of fecal bacteria, when O.J. got acquitted it was going to be Rodney King all over again), none of them were new. How could she have known he was suicidal? She was already sick of asking herself this, but it was a question that wouldn't go away. As she made her way out of the chapel, she hunched up behind the collar of her denim jacket and kept her eyes on the ground. She didn't notice Laura Katz coming up on her with longer than usual strides.

Laura had come to the service almost entirely to find Annabeth. Over the many months since they'd last spoken, she had come to regret their rift. And lately whenever she thought about starting her next picture, which she did almost hourly, she had begun to think about Annabeth's editorial skills, which had saved her ass on *Trouble Doll.* She understood that now, and no carefully worded note or earnest phone call was going to do the job of apology that was required. Showing up to acknowledge David's death, on the other hand, seemed appropriate. She'd seen enough to know that he had certainly loved Annabeth and that Annabeth had, in her own way, loved him back. Maybe Annabeth would be inclined to forgive Laura as a kind of voodoo-doll version of forgiving herself.

Stepping into the parking lot, during that moment when everyone's eyes were adjusting to the ridiculous brilliance of the still-early afternoon, Annabeth felt a hand on her forearm and turned. Seeing Laura's face was a shock, but she allowed the other woman to embrace her and soon found herself resting her cheek on Laura's shoulder. She was certain that she had never before hugged or been hugged by Laura, but she was now enfolded in Laura's arms as though they had a long history of loving embrace. It made Annabeth wonder how she would feel if Laura had been the one to die instead of David—for a moment, she even wished it, but the wish was halfhearted. It occurred to her then that the soft fabric under her cheek was one of Laura's fifty-dollar Japanese T-shirts and though no tears had yet fallen on it, if she remained there, they might. So she lifted her head.

"It's okay, it's washable," said Laura, and Annabeth had to laugh, in spite of everything.

Other mourners were making their way to their cars while the two women stood there, and some who passed concluded that the director and her editor were lovers, or had been. It was the kind of gossip that was sometimes as good as currency in the freelance marketplace of L.A. filmmakers, whether or not it was true.

Part 1

SMALL WORLD

1

Annabeth had first met Laura two years earlier, at a party in the Hollywood Hills where a lady elephant had been hired to entertain the guests. It was in the spring, or maybe late winter—at any rate, on a clear, pleasant evening like so many in Los Angeles. It was late and the elephant had been retired to the bottom of the driveway—available for photographs with anyone bored or stoned enough to step away from the hustle and into the cool, jasmine-scented night. The creature was wearing a gold lamé circus-performance outfit that might have convinced small children that she was gay and happy, an entertainer by choice. There were, however, no small children at the party.

"Stand back," the trainer said to Annabeth, as she wandered

down the hill. "She's about had it with this job, and she's got a temper."

"Really?" Annabeth asked, not meaning it. It seemed to her she could do nothing right at these insider parties—even the pachyderm was bored with her. She shouldn't leave the house when she was feeling this way; her neediness was on her like a stink. Are *you* my mother, Mrs. Mean Lady Elephant? Mr. Tortured Comedy Writer? Ms. Unbearably Arch Indie-Feature Producer?

"She doesn't like women much, either," the trainer added, assuming quite correctly that Annabeth—with her skulking stance and her formless T-shirt—was not anyone he needed to cultivate. Annabeth looked more closely at the elephant's enormous brow and tiny eye and felt defeated; nevertheless, she headed back up the driveway to the house. She could hear the giant animal's breathing and its anxious shifting of weight as she pulled herself uphill. Then the faint smell of hay, or something like it, triggered an emotion—regret? nostalgia?—and she turned to take a last look at the scene: tarted-up elephant, crabby guy in track suit, metal folding chair, BMW, Jeep, Mercedes, asphalt, cypress trees, enveloping lights of the L.A. basin.

Annabeth encountered Laura, dark-haired, black-clad, near the patio. It was almost midnight, but she was just arriving. She'd had to park a good way down Hollyridge Drive and so, though sleek, she was also somewhat sweaty.

"What's with the elephant?" she asked Annabeth.

"She's mean, apparently," said Annabeth, "and she hates women."

"You don't say," said Laura. "How did you manage to learn all that?"

And that was when Annabeth realized she was talking to Laura Katz. The Director. She'd seen *Two Chevrolets* at Sundance in '91 and had been following Laura's career in the trades ever since. Photographs had not done this woman justice, though. Golden skin on a taut armature, eyes impenetrably dark—she was Annabeth's opposite, her contrary. Successful people always turned out to be beautiful, too . . . well, successful women in Hollywood always turned out to be beautiful, or it seemed so to Annabeth, who was pretty when she tried to be—which was never.

Normally Annabeth would have been much too self-conscious to crassly accost this woman at a party, but it was already too late to get flustered, so she just answered Laura's question, providing additional details she'd heard earlier: that the elephant was a "picture" elephant ("You mean it's in the Screen Elephants Guild?" quipped Laura); that their host had hired it to be "the elephant in the room," so people would discuss it instead of his latest series— a wildly successful, utterly tasteless sitcom; and that the handler was peddling a wacky comedy about an experience he'd had during the Vietnam War with an elephant in a starring role.

"Too perfect!" said Laura.

"So you're Laura Katz," said Annabeth, immediately regretting her phrasing. Somehow, she had made it sound like an accusation.

"I am?" said Laura, half-teasing. "Sorry, I'm not used to being recognized—I guess I should be a little more gracious."

"That's okay," said Annabeth.

"Who are you?"

"Annabeth Jensen. I used to work with Janusz?"

"With Janusz!" said Laura.

"You were at AFI together."

"God, don't tell anyone that—they'll figure out how old I am."
But seeing Annabeth retract, she added, "Jesus, you're skittish—
were they serving paranoia weed in there or what?"

"No," said Annabeth, realizing a second too late that Laura's
question was rhetorical.

Laura walked ahead toward the patio's bamboo gate, but
Annabeth hadn't really made up her mind to go back to the pool
area. Before her visit to the elephant, she had found herself on
the outskirts of a conversation there that she'd found deeply disturbing—a conversation among sitcom writers. These were well-
bred, well-educated young men who had probably not fared well
in the social maelstroms of high school and college and who, in
their late twenties and early thirties, had come to Los Angeles to
exact their revenge. One aspect of their code of honor was that
none of them ever laughed out loud at a joke—his own, or anyone
else's.

The comedy guy Annabeth had had her eye on at the elephant
party was named Andrew something. She'd met him a few weeks
earlier at a Sunset Boulevard pub where he and his fellow wits
had a standing weekly get-together. While waiting for refills at the
bar that night, Andrew had told Annabeth he didn't really like
Guinness; he just drank it to seem cool. This had felt to her like
an intimate admission, although probably only because she was
drunk and he had the comedy-guy characteristic of looking mean-

ingfully into her eyes while cracking wise. In any case, he had charmed her, and when she saw him again that night at the party, she wandered over to stand nearby, joining an ad hoc audience that loosely ringed his circle of humorists.

At first, she felt perfectly content to be idling there. Then she noticed that the other bystanders were all men—the *next* generation of Ivy League comedy guys. She didn't like to stand out, and she hated the role of female acolyte. But when the wisecracking started to die down, she thought that the little knot of wits might untie itself enough for her to catch Andrew's eye. And, as it happened, he seemed to look directly at her as he spoke, answering a question she hadn't heard.

"Elizabeth? Fuckable?" he said, "I don't know . . . I think I'd really rather douse her in Sterno, sodomize her, and set her on fire."

Elizabeth was the girlfriend of their host, and Elizabeth—although blond and lovely—had a summa degree from Yale in Middle Eastern studies. Andrew's joke, as Annabeth ultimately parsed it, was about the unlikeliness of anyone ever doing any such thing to Elizabeth, especially anyone as fine-boned and circumspect as Andrew appeared to be. But, even among the comedy writers, in the laughless vacuum that was their air, this joke was not funny. At all. And that was the experience that had sent Annabeth down to visit the elephant in the first place. She had no desire to recount all this to Laura, but she *did* want to hold on to her new ally for as long as possible. When Laura reached out to open the gate that led to the pool area, Annabeth hesitated.

"What's the matter? Is there some guy in there that you slept with and shouldn't have?" Laura asked.

"Uh," said Annabeth, but Laura had already opened the gate and stepped through, leaving her no real choice but to follow.

Annabeth called Laura a few weeks later, after much anxious consideration. Was it too soon? Was she imposing? But they had had a good time together and Laura had volunteered her phone number. Still, Annabeth didn't really know how to call someone up just to chat, especially not someone so much further along in the business than she was. Ultimately, she decided to suggest lunch, but when she got Laura's answering machine, she choked and left only her name and number.

Laura called back the next day, which Annabeth took to be a sign of interest and enthusiasm. Usually, if she had the temerity to call a director about a job, it took at least three tries to get her call returned, often by an assistant. She didn't expect Laura to have an assistant ("Can you hold for Laura Katz?"), but she also didn't expect to get so rapid a response. However, Annabeth herself was out at the time of Laura's call—riding her bike along the bike path on the beach, which she did almost every afternoon when she couldn't stand her roommates for another second.

When the two women finally did connect, they had trouble finding a conversational stride—they'd both been drunk when they'd met, after all, and by then the elephant party was almost a month in the past. Laura had been the one to place the call. She'd just read in the trades that Becca Lawson, a hair-tossing bimbo with whom she'd gone to UCLA, had been made Meg Ryan's "head of production." This could have meant almost anything, but it activated the engine of envy in Laura's heart. Calling Annabeth was a way of rebalancing herself, making sure there were still people who wanted to be *her* the way she wanted to be . . . well, she didn't want to be Becca, she just wanted to make *Trouble Doll,* already. She wanted to see her own name in the trades, again. And so she called Annabeth and pretended that her movie was just a little bit closer to going forward than it in fact was.

"So, do you know Mia Goldman?" she asked Annabeth.

"A little. Not really. I mean, she's always been incredibly nice when I've called her about assisting, but I've never worked with her or anything."

"I'd heard she was interested in doing another indie project," said Laura.

Annabeth knew that Laura was shopping her next project around, hoping to make it independently. "Have you found a producer yet?"

"Actually, I met a guy I liked last week, Arthur Simpson?"

"Did he do *In the Soup?*"

"Unh-uh. He's been in London, at the BBC or something. But he's American—very midwestern and aw shucks. Disarming. He kind of reminds me of you, in fact."

Annabeth didn't know if this was a compliment or an insult. "Really?" she said.

"Anyway, he had some good ideas. Meanwhile, I'm still waiting for the writer to finish the draft we've been talking about . . . For. A. Year. It's so irritating."

Annabeth paused, wondering how to reintroduce the subject of lunch or whether she should. If Laura was thinking about Mia Goldman, there was no way she was going to hire Annabeth, who'd only just gotten her first full editing credit.

In the silence, Laura went back to the previous topic. "He was wearing a seersucker suit—when was the last time you saw one of those?"

"Wow," said Annabeth. Her father had worn seersucker suits. At least she thought she could remember him wearing one.

"Anyway, lunch," said Laura. "How about the week after next? Wednesday? I have a screening in the afternoon so maybe, I don't know, the Newsroom on Robertson?"

"Sure, that sounds great."

"But call me first," said Laura. "Friday? Just in case things get screwed up?"

Which, of course, they did.

2

David was then working in the recorded music collection at the Beverly Hills Public Library, a little-known pocket of hipsterism. The Moorish façade of the building looked very beautiful whenever Annabeth drove past, but she had been living in Los Angeles for over ten years before she first went inside. She was in her seventh month of unemployment after finishing *Golden State,* and she was always on the lookout for a good, cheap source of a few hours' entertainment. One afternoon when it was too windy for bike riding, she and her Honda found their way into the library's recently renovated parking structure.

While still working as Janusz's assistant on *Golden State,* Annabeth had spent many fruitless hours searching for a song that the scatterbrained editor had heard on the radio. He'd lost

the scrap of paper on which he'd written its name but could whis-
tle part of it, was reasonably sure the word *apple* was in the title,
and could think of no more perfect underscore for the chase sequence at the end of the movie. Abandoning her search for this
nameless, wordless tune had been a personal defeat for Annabeth. Though *Golden State* had long since been locked and timed
and prints struck with an old Steely Dan song doing the job of the
fugitive tune, she still had fantasies about identifying it and send-
ing a tape to Janusz at his new home in the Netherlands. But she
had never even *tried* the public library.

David, whose candid brown eyes belied the negativity of his
KILL ROCK STARS T-shirt, was the first person she talked to at the
Music Collection desk. He was immediately hooked by Annabeth's challenge. Especially after she whistled the tune for him,
leaning close, at library-whisper pitch. It was the most erotic
thing he had ever personally witnessed at the BHPL, or perhaps
anywhere. He got on the case immediately. The first step was to
brainstorm, with Annabeth, all the names of rock 'n' roll songs
with the word *apple* in them that they had heard of . . . or could
imagine. This was fun, but it didn't get them very far: After "Little Green Apples" and "Apple Scruffs" they were largely stumped.
They then amused each other for a while with hypotheticals:
"Bite the Apple!" said Annabeth. "Fruit of Eden!" rejoined David.
After a moment, he added, "Crabapple Jam?" Then they discussed the funny pronunciation of the name of the Simpsons'
schoolteacher, Mrs. Crabapple. Was it some pun they just
couldn't hear, some obscure reference too inside for the likes of
them? Anyway, after their brainstorming project sputtered, they
decided to divide and conquer: Annabeth would scan back issues

of *Rolling Stone* and David would visit the various Usenet sites he had recently learned to watch for music news.

They never found Janusz's song, which was, in fact, "All Apologies." (The *apple* clue had masked its identity even to David, who knew every note of every Nirvana song recorded to date.) But they bashfully agreed to meet at closing time at the peculiar Pico Boulevard bar called the Arsenal. It had real guns on the walls and a mock-Latin verse about buses full of livestock printed on the napkins. Heading west in their individual vehicles (David drove a brown 1984 Dodge Aries; Annabeth, a silver 1982 Honda Civic), they both listened to *All Things Considered* on KCRW, which was the only way either one of them ever really consumed national news.

They didn't go home together that night, mostly out of shyness, which may have been why their relationship lasted as long as it did. And when they did first lie down together two weeks later, the sun had not yet set. The plan had been for the two of them to meet at David's apartment, then head over to Sunset Boulevard for dinner before catching Morphine at the Troubadour, but David had news: at the last minute, he'd been offered a tryout at KCRW, subbing in the midnight-to-two A.M. slot. When Annabeth had stopped saying "Omigod" and "That's so amazing," he took her hand and led her to his bedroom.

Annabeth had never really had sober sex before—not with a new partner. She found it terrifying. All she could think about was what she might be doing wrong: Was it too soon to have arched her back that way? Should she have let him remove her clothes instead of tearing them off herself? Was her "what you see is what you get" cotton underwear a terrible mistake? Bright, late streaks of sunlight painted the bed as they lay there: everything was exposed. Later she punished herself over the memory of David recoiling when she began to nuzzle his balls. He was just ticklish, but Annabeth felt reproached and shamed for being so—curious? Willing? What? That imaginary misstep was only an instant in an otherwise happy half hour of coupling in David's clean, nearly empty bedroom, but in Annabeth's not-so-sunny soul it lived on for weeks.

Ordinarily, David would have been just as self-conscious, but he was in a rare moment of exaltation over his radio opportunity. In fantasy, he had already progressed rapidly beyond the two A.M. backwater and was behind the mike at *Morning Becomes Eclectic*, the station's flagship music show. (Its hosts interviewed anyone they wanted to; were consulted by journalists, scholars, record executives, and filmmakers; had comped seats at every live performance worth seeing; and never paid for drinks.) And because it was radio, looks were irrelevant. David was self-conscious about his small stature and weak chin, but he knew he had a melodious, affable voice. The die was cast, the cards were stacked, the time was right . . . In any case, he didn't notice anything amiss in Annabeth that afternoon. The skin on her back was so white, it looked like marble, or bone, or possibly even pearl.

When they got out of bed an hour later, it was the most polite and easygoing "morning after" Annabeth had ever experienced. David had none of the sheepishness or defensiveness men usually seemed to exhibit in that situation. He made them a nice snack of scrambled eggs with cilantro, gave her a clean towel to shower with, and generally behaved as though they were the oldest and

best of friends. He even walked her out to her car and, in the encroaching twilight, she looked west down Fifth Street and saw its
parade of towering palm trees.

"God, those are beautiful," she said. "I always notice them
from the freeway."

"Yeah, me too," said David. "You know they're full of rats."

"No way!" Annabeth loved this fact.

"Yeah, it's some urban mini-ecosystem, I guess."

"Rats in the trees—that should be the title of a song about
L.A."

"Oooh, so cynical."

"Yeah, well. Prove me wrong," said Annabeth, too quickly, and
immediately felt a patchy rush of blood in her cheeks. David
seemed not to notice, but she couldn't be sure. Maybe it sounded
casual enough—just a remark, not a long-held wish for a life of
tropical ratlessness, of palm trees and moonlight and a boyfriend
who looked her in the eyes when he kissed her.

3

Annabeth sat facing her wet dog of a reflection at Claude Hair
Studio and determined that complete metamorphosis was an un-
reasonable expectation, particularly since all she ever specified
was "You know, lose about an inch. Nothing foofy." She wasn't
even certain she'd said that much this time—it was a large part of
why she returned to Claude. He required little instruction and no
chitchat. Alone in his two-chair salon on an unfabulous segment
of Melrose Avenue, he approached every haircut with equal rigor,
passion, and self-direction. The few hairs he separated out for
each snip were part of a master plan to which he could mentally
refer without even seeming to rack focus. He was incredibly
painstaking, a little bit ominous, and the resulting haircut always
looked exactly the same. She wondered if she was as focused and

precise when editing—the activities were in some ways similar: intensely visual, conducted in the half dark, capable of almost infinite refinement. She kept hoping the artist in Claude would one day see through her diffidence and tell her she was ready to be transformed.

"Just cock your head a little bit to the . . . yeah." Claude regarded his work, pursed his lips, and dug back in.

In Los Angeles, most hair salons seemed to Annabeth like theatrical places—brightly lit boxes intended to be peered into from the street. They offered special costumes to their customers, played carefully considered sound tracks, crackled with gossip, and called everyone by her first name. She would have liked to be the sort of person who felt deserving, or at any rate plausible, in such places, but she was not. The few times she'd tried, she'd found herself racked with worries: how to politely reject the offer of extra conditioner or special blow-drying or whatever substance or service seemed imminent, who and how much to tip. She was always afraid that out of sheer meekness she would wind up with some grotesquely chic effect she could never carry off. In contrast, Claude Hair felt like a secret clubhouse, a low-rent speakeasy one needed a password to enter. Silhoetted in the front window was something that looked like a snake tree and turned out to be an antiquated permanent wave appliance. It cast creepy shadows on the wall behind Annabeth as headlights passed outside. The presence of the snake tree and Claude's eclectic mix tapes (Keely Smith, Yma Sumac, Ian Dury and the Blockheads) were the only clues she had to his actual personality. He was burly, fairly handsome, sometimes blond, and spoke as though he'd been taught English by Britons, or maybe even Afrikaners.

She had no idea whether he was straight or gay or both or neither, but she felt certain that cutting hair was not his real creative focus. She could picture him as a performance artist, an action painter, even a pianist or conductor—something requiring much bigger gestures than the ones he used while cutting hair. She was picturing him conducting *Einstein on the Beach* when he caught her eye in the mirror and smiled as though at some secret pleasure.

"You're done," he said.

Annabeth had been sitting still and silent for almost an hour and needed to go to the bathroom. She knew her way to the one in the back of the storefront bungalow, which looked like it belonged to someone's grandmother: 1930s pink-and-black tile. Once alone there, she stole a look at herself in the mirror and was disappointed. She wished she had the élan—the face, the clothes, the who-knew-what—to somehow animate the blond curtain that was her hair. Then she might look sleek and mod, like Vanessa Redgrave in *Blow-Up*—but she was just Vanessa's dowdy sister Lynn in *Georgy Girl*. She could hear a woman's muffled voice talking to Claude, up front; his next customer had arrived. She'd better go and pay.

Laura recognized Annabeth immediately. "No way!" she said. She was already sitting in Claude's chair and had been critically examining her own reflection.

"Look—come here." She extended her hand to Annabeth, who approached with something like wonder in her eyes: Laura went to *Claude*??? Laura *was* Vanessa Redgrave—well, Ali MacGraw, anyway. Laura swiveled the chair so her profile was reflected in the mirror and cocked her head at Annabeth. Claude stood back.

"I'm thinking about a skunk stripe," said Laura. "Just on the left, kind of Mrs. Robinson meets Susan Sontag. What d'you think?" Annabeth, smiling involuntarily at Laura's allusions, tried to envision the proposed change.

"Or we could do red," added Claude, looking up from the issue of *Film Threat* he was scanning. "You know, a little less of a direct quote."

Annabeth was stunned as much by Claude's sudden volubility as by the coincidence of seeing Laura seated in his chair. "Well," she said, "this is going to sound retarded, but you're so beautiful without it, I think it might be overkill."

"Ah, don't gild the lotus blossom," said Claude.

Laura, whose mother was Japanese, could have done without the lotus-blossom remark, but it was her policy not to comment on that kind of thing. Because her appearance was unplaceable and her last name was Katz (at least since she'd dropped the Ito and its trailing hyphen, in college), she preferred to remain ambiguous. Looking at Annabeth's reflection, she wondered about her outburst of flattery. It should have seemed too ingratiating to be credible, but Annabeth had said the words as though she had been to the factory where beauty was assembled—had even, herself, worked on the line—and knew firsthand what "beautiful" was and wasn't. Her eyes were no longer trained on Laura, though, and she seemed lost in thought about something else entirely. Laura found that she resented this withdrawal of admiration.

But Annabeth didn't need to stare at Laura to keep her foremost in mind. She had seen her almost imperceptible flinch at Claude's lotus-blossom comment and was now puzzling out what it might have meant. Laura's hair was shiny and coffee-colored and her eyes were gold, like cedar or tobacco. She might have had any number of ancestral sources: Gypsy, Filipino, Arab, Aleut— all equally exotic to Annabeth. Her own appearance was such that people assumed they knew everything about her at one glance: Scandinavian, Lutheran, probably from Minnesota, and therefore hardworking, reflexively "nice," and a tightwad, most of which was true. She felt Laura's gaze on her in the mirror and looked up.

"Guess I better pay up now," she said.

"You can leave it on the counter," said Claude.

Annabeth got out her checkbook and wrote out her payment. She didn't have to ask the price; it hadn't changed in three years. Claude walked over to the sink and beckoned to Laura.

"So what *are* we doing today?" he asked her.

"Just lose the gray," she said, taking her seat at the basin. "See you later, Annabeth."

"Bye," said Annabeth. Obviously, this was the wrong time to bring up the never-rescheduled lunch date.

4

Being invited to listen to David's recorded radio show was not the same thing at all as being given a mix tape, which was a courtship ritual that Annabeth understood. She watched as as he futzed with the tape-cueing mechanism.

"This is really the best example I have of what I'm about these days," David said, with his back to her. They were in the living room of his apartment, and his roommate, Ben, was away for the weekend. She had pictured them tumbling rapidly into the sack, but after being seated on the couch and then abandoned in favor of seemingly endless stereo ministrations, she recalibrated. From David's jerky gestures, she could tell that he was nervous. And there was a portentousness in the way he then turned and waited for her to settle in before he hit "play." Clearly this was not all about sex. It was early in the day to be drinking, but she was grateful for the cold beer he had set in front of her. She leaned back into the cushions and pulled her hair off the back of her neck, conscious that David was watching her with an intensity that should have been exciting but wasn't. The futon couch was surprisingly comfortable and clean and she wondered if Ben (she hadn't met him yet) was a homosexual.

"Ready?" he asked, and she nodded and shut her eyes as the recorded David introduced himself and his show, which was to be "a meditation on breaking the rules." His radio voice was deep and soft, intensely sexy. She tried to imagine what she would think about this guy if she had heard him on the radio first, and only met him later. Definite crush. The first song on the tape was a noisy blast of punk, the kind of thing she hated. She tried to look like she was enjoying it, but two and a half minutes was too long to keep that up. Ultimately, she opened her eyes and revealed what she hoped was a not too painfully beseeching face to David. He nodded disinterestedly.

She had assumed that deejaying was like editing, that it was about assembling and adjusting parts that are meant to fit and also about removing whatever is foreign to the whole. Now she sensed that she had been mistaken. Perhaps they had nothing in common at all. Then the second song began—it was Nina Simone singing "Don't Explain." But after her initial relief, Annabeth's mind again became critical. He was treating his "theme" of rule breaking too obviously: angry punks, jarring juxtapositions, adultery . . . She had wanted David to surprise her. But maybe that just was too much to have expected and, anyway, this was only minute five of the twenty-five minute tape.

David knew what she was thinking, more or less. These first two tracks, though dear to him in various ways, were mainly there to draw fire from the listener, to get rid of the obvious ideas so he could start playing with the subtler ones. Simone's growling lullaby would soon give way to "Memo from Turner," and Ry Cooder's sly, Oriental-carpet figure of an introduction would unroll for Annabeth, coax her into the song, and then transform itself into a freight train. And, sure enough, by the time Jagger's vocal stepped in, David could see that Annabeth had forgotten all about the show's putative theme and was just completely listening.

Annabeth had never heard this particular Stones' song, and in perhaps a more unusual omission had never seen the movie *Performance,* from which it comes. At first she wasn't even certain that the voice singing belonged to Mick Jagger, but its taunting rock 'n' roll intimacy triggered a torrent of high school memories—days and nights with Trevor, the rich kid who'd been her boyfriend when she was seventeen. His older brothers had left him a trove of records and a marijuana connection in the Cities, which, together, had made the Rasmussen house Annabeth's refuge for days a time. Trevor had actually been the one who'd convinced her to apply to schools out of state, and so had saved her life, she now realized. She hadn't thought about him in years, but the music had reanimated him, from his sarcastic smile to his filthy Levi's. She blushed, thinking of the time they'd had sex under the piano in the never-used room the Rasmussens called "the library." He'd told her she was beautiful then, and she'd believed him.

When David's voice again emerged from the speaker, Annabeth was caught off guard. She took a long, head-back swig of beer to deflect his notice from the blush in her cheeks and to distract herself from the warmth in her vulva.

"In my family," David's radio voice said, "we don't eat pork, buy German cars, or serve cocktails, but we don't light candles or pray either. It's like, if we don't actually identify ourselves as Jews, no one can ever use our Jewishness against us. Which is pretty funny, considering the past two thousand years. But maybe that's why we think God will give us a pass on the rituals—or maybe it's a test, a dare, *Hit us again, you big bully, go ahead.* But I grew up in southern California, I went to class barefoot in high school, ordered lobster Cantonese every Sunday night, knew the words to 'Subterranean Homesick Blues' before I could say *Baruch atah Adonai* . . . So, to whom should I address my complaints? Or should I complain at all?" Annabeth didn't entirely understand this speech, but she wanted to and was trying to formulate a question for David when he took the beer bottle from her hand and set it aside, then kissed her.

Driving home the next day, Annabeth went over the "date" in her head. She put a lot of stock in the theory that within the first few weeks of any affair, lovers show each other the characteristics that will one day upend the relationship. The preceding afternoon's enforced listening experience certainly seemed to have contained pertinent revelations. Vanity? A certain didacticism? But neither of these were deal breakers in her book. She just wanted to avoid mistakes she'd made before: guys who didn't really want her around once they had her. Still, she had a feeling that she had received a warning, if only she could decode it. The content of the radio show had seemed mostly innocuous to her, in spite of its advertised theme. The Jewish stuff was a little bit bothersome, but only because it underlined the absence of cultural or family identity in her own life. She kind of liked the idea of going out for Chinese food every Sunday night with David's parents, though. She wondered how long they would have to be together before he would invite her along.

In fact, after only six weeks, Annabeth and David moved in together in Venice. A high school friend of David's was giving up the perfect house, and together they could afford the rent. It was a bungalow on Nowita Court, a filled-in canal too narrow for automobile traffic, a "walk street." This corridor was densely planted, which made it shady and cool in the summer but also unusually dark for southern California. A short walk west, across Electric Avenue, they had a cappuccino joint (Abbot's Habit), two decent restaurants (Hal's and Capri), and Babe Brandelli's Brig, a skeevy bar with pool tables where guys like David could go to feel less suburban. The ocean, though invisible, was nearby—this was apparent in the density of the morning fog and the frequent appearance of darkly tanned young men wandering back to their cars in the early mornings, their black rubber skins half-shucked. Annabeth felt about seeing surfers in her neighborhood the way other L.A. newcomers felt about having fruit trees in their yards—now, she was living the dream.

The little bungalow had been built as a summer retreat so, though charming, it was tiny, underinsulated, and short on closet space. It had five rooms, one of which they used mostly for storage: two bicycles; David's ski equipment, tennis racket, and reel-to-reel tape player; Annabeth's student films, many boxes of books, scripts, and records; two trunks; and five suitcases. It drove them both crazy that they were giving up a whole bedroom to this crap, but neither of them could figure out what else to do with it, so the room remained an indoor garage. The rest of the house offered a living room (complete with fireplace), a dining room, a rickety kitchen, and the "master" bedroom, which just about accommodated their full-sized mattress and two mismatched dressers—his and hers. David's was incredibly neat and had framed pictures on it showing his family at his sister's wedding, his long-deceased childhood dog (Brownie, a standard poodle), and an awkward teenage David standing in front of his first car, an AMC Gremlin. Annabeth's dresser usually had at least one open drawer. As for family pictures, her mother had systematically burned them all when Annabeth was sixteen, which was when Eva had finally accepted that her husband's last disappearance was permanent.

Denise, the only friend from Duluth with whom Annabeth had kept up, had pointed out more than once that Annabeth's childhood must have been harder than she let on, what with the mostly absent alcoholic father, the raging mother, the clueless older brother, and the "creepy" old house in the middle of nowhere. "And what about you?" Denise would ask on the phone, always with the same tone, implying that certainly something dramatic or momentous might need to be unloaded, but Annabeth always brushed off this question. She had no gruesome memories; there was always food on the table and clean laundry in the drawer. Even now, although she barely spoke to her mother, she would never have called her "bad" or "mean."

In truth, Eva Jensen had gone a quiet kind of crazy when

Annabeth was an adolescent. As with all of his earlier disappearances, she had initially dealt with Gus's final departure with equanimity. She continued to go to work, buy the groceries, pay the bills, and appear normal to the neighbors. Even after a year had passed and twelve-year-old Annabeth had begun asking her to stop it, she still set a place for him at the dinner table and still saved his mail, unopened, though it had long since overflowed the tray on top of his desk. She went on buying him birthday presents and rotating his winter and summer suits from closet to closet for almost four years. Annabeth could remember throwing her trig textbook across the kitchen and screaming, "He's never coming back!" at the top of her lungs. Loud enough so even the neighbors could have heard, she thought the next day, feeling humiliated. But the confrontation had ended with Eva strangely composed, only Annabeth in tears, and her brother, Jeff, upstairs in his room with the stereo turned up loud. Ultimately, Annabeth found the easiest thing was to pretend that her father had never existed. When new acquaintances asked about him, she began to say, "I never knew him," which, all things considered, seemed perfectly true.

Occasionally, in the months following his first tryout, David was called to fill in on late-night shifts at KCRW, but these calls always came at the last minute and there was never any subsequent comment about how he had done—he suspected no one at the station really listened to the radio at that hour, anyway. He presumed his audience was mostly composed of club kids and late-shift film technicians and he felt confident about his ability to provide entertainment to them, but he still very much wished one of the station's grown-ups would give him a little notice, even criticism—something to let him know the job might one day be real, and was not just some weird dream he kept having.

"You have to give that up," Annabeth told him. "Nobody in the entertainment business gives meaningful commentary on the work of the wannabes. It's like an unwritten rule." Had Janusz Zielinski been there to overhear this remark, he would have called her a liar, but they were alone on the back steps. The afternoon air was warm and, for a change, the inky smell of the ocean was superseding the pong of cat feces that haunted their alleyway.

"It's not the entertainment business," argued David. "It's National Public Radio."

"Right," said Annabeth. But she heard herself sounding like the cigarette-smoking old souse at the end of the bar and decided to dial it down a bit.

"Okay," said David, having taken her silence as an instruction to think again. "So music is part of the entertainment business . . . I can admit that. But why do you think it's against the rules for anyone to acknowledge that I exist?"

She looked at him fondly, the reddish-gold hairs on his forearm lit by the raking light, his downcast eyes, his fat peasant's feet. The white stripes where his rubber thongs blocked the sun looked particularly vulnerable to her just then.

"You exist," she said. "But the thing is, they're all looking up at whoever *they* need affirmation from. No matter how far up they get, there's always another daddy."

He nodded, peeking out from under his shaggy hair at his really very new girlfriend, Annabeth. She was right. She often was when it came to this kind of thing. He was lucky, he knew it, and was terrified that she knew it, too.

Although she talked tough about the entertainment business, Annabeth was just as tentative about her right to occupy a place in it as David was. She had recently come to the end of her unemployment payments and was feeling increasingly uneasy about watching her money market account balance dip below ten thousand dollars, which it was about to do. She knew that David was probably good for more than his income, but she didn't want to ask him. (Indeed, David's finances were a sensitive subject: his mother had been sent to Paris before the war with all of her parents' assets. Neither she nor the family friends who had raised her had ever drawn from those accounts, or even really looked at them, except to make them over into a trust for David and his sister. By the time of David's college graduation, it was already worth several million dollars. He claimed to have no compunction about spending this legacy, and had sometimes used it recklessly for stereo equipment and live performance tickets but, in truth, the family money cast as long a shadow over his life as the tiny Jews to whom it had once belonged.)

Since moving to the house on Nowita Court, Annabeth had had a few vague conversations with former coworkers about features possibly starting up in the next few months, but nothing had panned out. She told herself that it was normal to have an uneven period when you jumped up a level (as she had, almost involuntarily, on Janusz's departure). That was why she kept such a substantial savings cushion in the first place. But she also knew that she was not yet "really" an editor and that her job-hunting efforts had been insufficient—she hated networking. She was certain that all her peers believed Janusz had given her the credit on *Golden State* only to reward her for the four years of groveling they assumed she had done as his assistant. But Janusz had never asked her to pick up his dry cleaning or babysit for his kids. Moreover, she really had cut most of the picture. After Corey Hunt, their insecure young director, had come into the cutting room one day waving five pages of voice-over narration he'd written the night before, Janusz had lost it. He was fifteen years older than the Idiot (as they called him), ten times as smart, and twenty times as knowledgeable about cinematic storytelling. Moreover, Janusz's wife was threatening to leave him if he canceled another weekend plan. "There is no focking way I'm shooting down my marriage so the Idiot-boy can make five new versions of the same movie with the same focking footage!" he concluded. In the end, Annabeth had been the one to recut the picture: first as a road movie, then as a fish-out-of-water comedy, and finally as a buddy picture. "Now you have a complete portfolio," Janusz told her, by phone from Amsterdam, where he and Agniezka were in the process of moving. "Welcome to ninth circle of hell."

Annabeth had been working for Janusz for five years when he left. Even between projects, they had spoken on the phone every few weeks. He had seen her through three apartments, two boyfriends, one race riot, and two impacted wisdom teeth. In the long dry spell that followed *Golden State,* she often wished that she could just go back to being his assistant.

5

Laura and Annabeth coincidentally ran into each other one more time that summer, at a women's networking brunch in Laurel Canyon. It was the kind of thing neither of them usually went to, but Laura was shopping for a producer for *Trouble Doll* and Annabeth was looking for an editing job, and so there they were. The difference between them was clear, however: Laura felt like she had something to offer, while Annabeth felt like she was looking for a handout.

On her way there, at the treacherously steep corner of La Cienega and Sunset, Annabeth had a momentary vision of her car rolling backward down the hill, gaining momentum, and crashing into the busy intersection at Santa Monica Boulevard. She'd never heard of this happening, but the sheer physics of the situation seemed to guarantee that someday it would and, when it did, the projectile would certainly be a car like hers, with old brakes and old gears and a spotty record of repair. She disliked driving in the hills. The absurd, delighted street names, mazelike layouts, and enthusiastic plantings always seemed like an open invitation to disaster. If God existed and had any self-respect at all, he would have to take a swipe at this ridiculous display. But the folded and crumpled stretch of landscape that made up Laurel, Nichols, and Beachwood Canyons was where the movie business hipoisie tended to roost. Annabeth told herself she only had to stay at the brunch for five minutes. If there was no one there that she knew, she could turn around and go home. If she stayed for an hour, she would stop at the Brentwood Country Mart on the way home and reward herself with a frozen espresso.

As her car climbed into the canyon, the shadows thrown by the bright sunshine shifted with the breeze. Her destination was a small, pink ranch-style house on Wonderland Avenue. It had the kind of anonymous exterior that told Annabeth it was probably a rental. This was a detail that she'd learned to take note of in Los Angeles, along with whether someone's groceries came from Ralphs or Gelson's, whether they "self-parked" or used the valets, and whether a washed-out-looking cotton T-shirt had come from Fred Segal or the Gap.

The brunch was already well under way when Annabeth entered through the unlocked front door. The living room was full of young women in flower-print dresses or the aforementioned Fred Segal T-shirts worn with linen shorts. Annabeth was the only person in the room wearing Levi's and just about the only one not sporting a hair scrunchie. (They didn't stay in her hair; it was too straight and thin.) She looked like she always looked, and she hoped that was okay because she didn't know how to look any other way. The best she could do was to substitute a clean white T-shirt for her usual laundered-to-near-transparency black one and to don her "good" shoes, which were cowboy boots. She smiled abstractedly as she headed for the buffet table while surreptitiously scanning the party in search of a familiar face. While doing this, she overheard two D-girls gossiping about David Mamet, who had just doctored a script for the director or producer who employed one of them.

Annabeth had learned about D-girls when she worked in cutting rooms on the Fox lot with Janusz. "De-welopment," he had explained, "is what they call buying scripts and rewriting until they are too bad to be movies." The girls themselves tended to be pleasant and well educated, but whenever Annabeth wound up talking to one—in the commissary or at duplication services—the girl's eyes would glaze over as soon as she realized Annabeth worked in "post." She would not have stopped to listen to the D-girls at the party that day, except the name David Mamet interested her. She had once heard him speak on a panel and he had been both both wise and hilarious. The conversation she overheard at the networking brunch went something like this:

D-girl with ponytail: "I can't even tell you how much we paid."

D-girl with big diamond ring: "Of course not." A polite pause; then: "Two-fifty?"

No denial from Ponytail, just a smile, a beat, and the "keep going" gesture. "This is unbelievable. Listen. We get this envelope from FedEx last week and the script's in it. I mean the *same exact* copy that I sent him six weeks ago. No note, no nothing. So I flip through it? And eventually—like around page thirty-five or some-thing—I come to some writing. In Sharpie! He wrote on it with magic marker! There were maybe twenty changes in the whole thing, some cuts, a few words here and there, and they're like *scrawled*."

"No way! What did Bill say?" Bill, Annabeth surmised, was Ponytail's director, producer, or actor employer.

" 'Fucking brilliant!' "

The D-girls stared at one another with eyebrows circumflexed. It was as though each was waiting for the other to betray some sign of whether or not Bill's comment was to be understood as a joke. It defied all of their expectations and training. Annabeth watched the wheels turn. Obviously, whatever Bill did was right in this case. And it was received wisdom that Mamet was a ge-nius—Pulitzer Prize. So: half a million dollars for a few dozen strokes of Sharpie? Money well spent!

Laura had overheard this little conference, too, as it turned out. Her eyes met Annabeth's over the heads of the mystified D-girls and they both had to turn away before they fell apart laughing. A few moments later, near the fruit salad, Annabeth felt someone grab her arm. "Fucking brilliant!" Laura repeated and they laughed again, and then took their plastic dishes outside and sat side by side on a flowered chaise longue positioned to have a view across the canyon.

"So what are you doing here?" asked Annabeth, to whom the idea that Laura would ever have to network seemed absurd on its face.

"Looking for crew—department heads, maybe an editor."

Did she remember that Annabeth was an editor? Was she

being purposefully coy? Annabeth knew from the *Weekly* article that Laura herself had started out as an editor. Jerry Greenberg, who cut *The French Connection,* had hired her when she was "just a kid," she'd told the reporter. Also according to that article, which Annabeth had reread twice since their first meeting, Laura was only five years older than she was. "But don't you do your own cutting?" she asked.

"Last time, that didn't work so well," said Laura.

Annabeth couldn't quite bring herself to say, "What about me?" because she couldn't quite tell whether Laura was teasing her. In the article, Laura'd said she'd be "boiled in oil" before she saw a film of hers cut on a digital system, that cutting a movie without handling the celluloid itself was like writing a symphony without touching a musical instrument. She must have had to eat those words by now, but still they meant that she understood the craft, that she wouldn't expect her editor to recut a ghost story as a caper film. Annabeth's heart was beating fast—should she say something? But maybe it was better not to push.

"So, seen any good movies lately?" she asked instead. This question got them through the rest of the brunch—they had pro-foundly similar taste. Martin Bell's *American Heart* was the first common bond, but their shared guilty pleasure in *The Fabulous Baker Boys* sealed the deal. "Who knew it was still possible to make a musical?" said Laura. "Who knew it was still possible to make a romance?" said Annabeth, nodding wistfully.

Below where they sat, a stretch of Lookout Mountain Avenue's asphalt was visible, and as their conversation paused, a Western Exterminator van drove by. Mounted on its roof was a papier-mâché gentleman caught in the act of walloping a rodent with a giant black mallet—he looked like the Monopoly banker. It was a hilarious thing when you saw it on the freeway, but it seemed even funnier rustling by among the climbing vines and wind chimes of Laurel Canyon. As the van passed from sight, Laura said, "There's this movie . . ." and Annabeth said "*Last Night at the Alamo!*" They exchanged a glance of stunned hilarity as they realized they'd both seen and appreciated the same obscure little movie. (*Alamo*'s main character, an off-duty exterminator, drives a pickup truck fitted with a pathetically homemade-looking pair of vinyl rat ears.) For Annabeth, this moment seemed magical. Not only could Laura see the humor in the Western Exterminator truck, she understood why Annabeth sometimes went into the room with the Acmade edge coder just to smell its fumes—*and* she was the director of *Two Chevrolets*! It all made her so happy that she drove home chorusing along with U2 on the radio. As the glittering ocean came into view over the hill at Fourth Street, Annabeth had the rare, exalted feeling that she was in the right place at the right time.

6

While jobless and first adjusting to life with David, Annabeth began to have a recurring nightmare. In it, she was at a sewing machine, piecing together the skin of an elephant. The skin was bloody and hard to maneuver, and the needle on the sewing machine was dull. There was a deadline to complete the job—she was not going to make it—and periodically she had to ask herself if the elephant was even dead or if it was its persistent life that made it so difficult to sew. Her hands and arms were slick with blood to the elbows. When she woke up from this dream the first time, she started to describe it to David but grew ashamed when she realized how ghoulish it sounded. She didn't want him to think that was what her subconscious was really like. But he

seemed not to mind at all, asking her to go into detail about everything. He even asked her how it smelled, which upset her. Because it did smell; it smelled like the basement of the house she'd
grown up in: bruised apples, mildew, and kerosene. She wouldn't
have had to know that if he hadn't asked.

Most of the movie-business people Annabeth knew well—the
crew members and postproduction staff—had hobbies. Between
jobs, they gardened or golfed, made paintings, threw pots, danced,
cooked, knitted, wrote poetry, and worked out. They all worked
out. Annabeth's hobbies were going to the movies, reading, walking, and riding her bike on the boardwalk. Being near the ocean
mattered to her for some reason she could never put her finger
on. It wasn't as though she ever swam in it. In any case, she didn't
really have enough to do with herself while unemployed, and she
and David began to get in each other's way. He was working two
afternoons a week at the library and also occasionally subbing at
KCRW but he was home an awful lot, and their house was all of
a thousand square feet.

The area of their most heated disputes was the living room:
David wanted to use the stereo for listening to music; Annabeth
wanted to watch videos. David was willing to use headphones—
in fact, he preferred to—but Annabeth was not willing to watch
movies with the blinds open. This irritated David, who was ob-
sessed with getting "enough" sunlight (but had never explained to
Annabeth why he believed this was so important, because that
would have required telling her the story of his teenage depression in all its disturbing detail). For the most part it was a silent
battle, with David angling the blinds and repositioning the TV to

address the glare problem that he assumed to be Annabeth's underlying concern, and Annabeth closing the blinds as soon as he left the room because it wasn't about the glare, it was about immersion.

When David came home from the farmers' market one Wednesday morning and found Annabeth sitting in the dark, already well into *Nights of Cabiria,* he left the front door wide open before carrying his shopping bags into the kitchen. He knew he'd get a reaction, but he didn't know what it would be. He'd never intentionally provoked her before. In fact, they'd never really had a fight.

Annabeth sprang forward like a toy goblin but remained silent, telling herself he would return and close the door after he'd put down the shopping. She picked up the remote control but didn't pause the tape. Then David stuck his head through the doorway and said, "It's ten in the morning—what are you doing?"

"I'm watching a movie, obviously."

"You're lying on the couch in the dark like an invalid."

"I'm watching a Fellini movie. I happen to be lying down. What's your problem?"

David shrugged dramatically, implying that her reaction was unduly harsh. Annabeth looked back at the movie but after a few seconds found that she was too irked to focus. She stopped the tape again, got up, and went into the kitchen. A bunch of wildflowers was lying on the kitchen table—pink and lavender ones she couldn't name. David was taking things out of the refrigerator and lining them up on the counter: jars of jam and hot sauce; quart yogurt containers full of festering remnants; a brittle, translucent slab of cheese. The food he'd bought at the market, in filthy canvas bags originally obtained at Trader Joe's, remained on the table beside the rapidly wilting flowers.

"Is something the matter?" asked Annabeth.

"The refrigerator is disgusting," David said.

"Not a big surprise—neither of us cleans it."

David slammed the fridge door and turned on her. "And whose fault is that?"

"Ours?" Annabeth paused for a moment and tried to regroup. "What are you so mad about?"

"I ran into Danny Kaplan at the market," he said, sitting down at the table, apparently changing the subject. "With his wife and their new baby. Isabel. She's adorable." Annabeth couldn't remember who Danny Kaplan was. Some half-famous musician, most likely. She could never keep their names straight. "They just got back from Paris," David continued.

Then she remembered: Kaplan was a production designer who had gone to high school with David. "Well, I bet his wife lets him watch all the movies he wants," she said, not realizing her poisonous implication until she'd already said the words.

"I'm your fucking wife?" David yelled.

Annabeth just stood there in the doorway.

"Are you expecting me to bear your children for you, too?" he added.

Annabeth went back to the couch, where she sat down, blinking. *That was an uncalled-for remark,* she thought. It should have hurt like hell. The thing was, she had no intention of having children. After a moment or two, she heard him resuming his activity in the kitchen—the sounds of items hitting the trash container, water running, the garbage disposal doing its job. Flummoxed, she returned to the movie. After backing it up a few feet, she pretended she had found her way back into the story. Instead, the movie ran, and Annabeth's thoughts ran alongside it. She'd never wanted to be a mother. Mothers were trapped, enslaved creatures. But David probably *did* want children. His parents wanted grandchildren, certainly. So what was she doing moving in with this guy, playing house? When, in the movie, Cabiria packed up her scant belongings to go off with a guy she's just met, you knew she was making a mistake. But you also loved her for her bravery, her faith. It was a nearly perfect movie and the sequence then starting, where Cabiria spends the night in a movie star's apartment, was Annabeth's favorite part.

As soon as David left the house the next day, Annabeth called her friend Denise in Ann Arbor. Denise had become a pediatrician, a wife, and a mother in the time it had taken Annabeth to go from apprentice editor to first assistant. She was not exactly Annabeth's version of Danny Kaplan, but only because the two women were and had always been close friends.

"I fucked up," said Annabeth, after catching up on Denise's latest doings. It didn't take that long, because Denise knew she was being called for a reason. "I don't know why I always do this. He's basically the nicest guy I've ever slept with."

"Do what?" said Denise.

"Turn into a shrew."

"Funny, you don't look shrewish." This was an old joke from high school, and it comforted Annabeth just to hear it repeated. Annabeth's shrewishness had been one of her mother's ever-ready explanations for why her father had gone away.

"I just don't know how to be in a couple—I never have."

"Couples have fights; it's not the end of the world."

"Yeah, but . . ."

"But yours was worse?"

Annabeth smiled wryly, accepting this truth. "I was mean," she said. "I insulted his manhood."

"Did you apologize?"

"Yes."

"Did he accept your apology?"

"Yes."

"Then you're done," said Denise. "Let it go."

Yeah, right, thought Annabeth. Sometimes Denise's wisdom seemed to verge on smugness. She could never quite believe she had a close friend who actually said the things printed on bumper stickers. There were a lot of AA bumper stickers in Los Angeles, Gothic letters printed on foil, like the logos of '80s metal bands: "Easy Does It," "One Day at a Time," "Powerless." Why would anyone want to be powerless? And yet Denise was the only person Annabeth had ever met who seemed unequivocally to love her life—and not in a saccharine way either. Once, when Annabeth had visited Denise at college, she'd allowed herself to be dragged along to an Al-Anon meeting in Madison: a room full of buttoned-up Swedes and Norwegians. They all looked normal enough at first but turned out to be human train wrecks. Annabeth recognized that there had been alcohol abuse in her family, probably for generations, but it was nothing like the Mom's-blacked-out-on-the-couch-again nightmare of Denise's childhood. Nevertheless, when Annabeth's life got bad, she always called

Denise. Denise was the only one who was ever able to make Annabeth feel better.

A week later, David was given the regular midnight-to-three Tuesday and Thursday slot at KCRW. The pay was ridiculously low, but at least it was a steady check, and KCRW had a commitment to deep and varied music programming, so it was an amazing opportunity. He called his segment *Old Brown Show,* which *was* a pun on the little-loved Beatles track but was *not* a sly implication about the importance of African and black influences in popular music. Well, not consciously or intentionally—not any more than the Beatles tune's name had been. Of course, people assumed it was and told David it was "brave" and "witty," and these observations made him uncomfortable. He put everything he had into the show. Seeing his name on the program grid in the station's monthly newsletter the first time nearly made his heart stop—his parents and all their friends got that newsletter, too. Take that, Danny Kaplan.

David's taste in music encompassed various chapters of pop, soul, funk, psychedelic rock, art rock, R&B, and even the occasional instance of rap, but his concept for *Old Brown Show* was to play new music that *felt* old, and that was all he'd meant by the name. He'd pictured an ankle-high brown blucher with its sole partially unstitched: a hillbilly shoe, tapping out a steady rhythm. He'd pictured that image on a compilation CD that the station would sell at the annual fund-raiser. He'd pictured himself getting to meet and interview guys like Beck and Kurt Cobain. Kurt would certainly "get" what he was trying to do.

But he soon found that the three hours he spent doing the show were the loneliest, weirdest, most relentlessly painful hours he had ever spent doing anything. He'd had radio shows before—at Vassar, and in Lake Placid, where he'd lived for a while after college. But people had *listened* to those shows—they told him so, and he believed them. In Los Angeles, people claimed to listen but he could tell they were lying—the same way they lied about having read the book discussed on *Bookworm,* or having seen the brilliantly reviewed Turkish film that played for exactly one week at the Royal. Liza Richardson, who was his lead-in, always did a lovely job of introducing him and he always showed up wildly overprepared with liner notes and library books and clever associations, but he still felt himself fall into a state of helpless ineloquence as soon as the ON AIR light was illuminated—even when the music was playing. For the first few days, he phoned Annabeth during the music sets, but it *was* the middle of the night and he could tell she was lying in bed half asleep and resented being made to talk on the phone.

In reality, many people other than Annabeth were listening to *Old Brown Show,* and no people—including Annabeth—found it dull or disappointing. To them, David Bronstein seemed like a droll, understated dude they'd like to know better. And for no real reason beyond the lateness of the hours at which he broadcast, they assumed he was someone largely immune to music business fame-mongering and hype. When he introduced one of his discoveries, a song by the band Papas Fritas (which he pronounced in Californian iambs: *pahpuz freeduss*), he commented, "Well, I guess it's freed me, too, 'cause here I sit talking to the void. On the other hand, maybe I have Marlo Thomas to thank for that . . ." For people David's age, the *Free to Be . . . You and Me* reference was a gimme. It was that kind of almost random association that made his on-air sensibility so appealing—he was an outsider's insider, self-conscious to the point of self-parody.

7

A trio of stores called American Rag occupied the middle of the block of La Brea Boulevard between First and Second Streets, and its three distinct storefronts offered new and used fashions, very expensive shoes, and housewares, respectively. Crammed into the back of the housewares store was a café that sold salads and quiches and various types of coffee, all served by unusually handsome French waiters. These men, along with certain very expensive tea towels and the "et Cie" that no one ever pronounced in the name of the place, were the only trace of Frenchness on the premises, but the shopaholics of greater Los Angeles seemed to find these elements sufficiently exotic to justify spending fifteen dollars on an omelette with a tiny, wilted sprig of frisée on the side.

Annabeth rarely shopped in this part of town for anything—it was far from where she lived, and she was not someone who paid much attention to fashion. Nevertheless, during the months of idleness since her last job, she'd begun to notice that at unemployment, the Santa Monica Public Library, the Nuart cinemas, and Abbot's Habit café, young hipsters had started wearing Hush Puppies—in bright colors. She had also learned that the store that sold these shoes was just down the street from American Rag, which was why she had been the one to suggest the associated café to Laura as the location for their much-postponed first lunch. She thought that Laura might be the sort of person who would tell her it was okay to spend fifty-five dollars on shoes even though she was unemployed. Over *jambon et fromage,* however, Laura began telling Annabeth about *Trouble Doll,* and Annabeth soon forgot all about the red shoes. She was flattered to death when Laura asked for her advice on how to manage her ongoing difficulties with the script's author, a woman named Ramona Engel.

"She's not very smart," said Laura, "but there's something really cool about the script—it's funny and sad at the same time."

"That's my favorite thing in movies." said Annabeth. "Did you ever see *Signs of Life?*"

Laura dropped her jaw theatrically. "That Gypsy! The king!"

"I know. The way he dances at the end just kills me."

"And that car shot, with the clouds of dust?"

"Fucking Werner Herzog—why is he so inconsistent?"

Laura laughed. "God, Annabeth, you're so cool. Why can't *you* be my writer?"

Annabeth laughed too. She was thrilled by Laura's remark.

After her grin died down she thought to ask, "What do you mean, she's not very smart?"

"She just doesn't seem to get that movies have their own momentum and logic. Anytime I want to change something about the main character, she starts whining about how that's not the way it really was and I just don't know enough about how people think in Nebraska, Kansas, whatever—as though anyone is interested in the True Story of Ramona Engel."

"So it's autobiographical?"

"Isn't everything?"

"Well, I'm not a writer . . ."

"Do you want to read it for me? I really think it's just a tweak away from being ready to go."

"What's it about?"

"I think it's about striving," said Laura. "And the culture of fame." Annabeth nodded but found this to be a completely opaque answer. Laura saw that she'd lost her audience and began again: "It's about a girl from the Midwest who comes to L.A. to find fame and fortune and winds up dead on the side of the road."

"Not a comedy, then," said Annabeth.

Laura smiled and continued: "She's a stripper, and she lives with this guy Trip, a loser—he's got a drug problem, he can't keep a job. And she borrows money from her boss to get Trip's car fixed after he totals it. Meanwhile, she meets this actor at the strip club. He's, like, a little bit famous from TV and he tells Bunny— that's her name, I love that—that he's going to set her up with his agent and get her an audition and all that. Anyway, long story short: her boss starts wondering where his money is and Bunny starts sleeping with the actor and . . . you know, the ditch."

"Is she a moron, or do we like her?"

"Oh, no, we totally like her. We have to."

"Right," said Annabeth, wondering if that would be possible for her, given what she'd just heard.

"Malkovich might be interested in playing the agent," said Laura. "It's a cameo, but that will help us get a real actress for Bunny."

"Wow," said Annabeth, thinking, *She said "us."*

"So, I'd love to hear what you think."

Annabeth drained the last tiny slurp of café au lait under the foam in her cup and entered a brief fantasy of herself cutting a sequence with John Malkovich in it. She had a feeling he was one of those actors whose faces never went dead, who always had something new to bring. She would love to work on something with someone that good in it. She picked up the dessert menu—she didn't want Laura to see whatever was going on on her own face and she feared it was transparent. Once, Janusz had shown Annabeth how, just by letting a shot run an extra dozen frames or so, he made Ellen Barkin's vulnerable-looking smile become that of a likely betrayer. The suspicion never paid off, and the character's potential duplicity wasn't even in the script; it just made the scene, and therefore the movie, more interesting. Sometimes David would look at her a little too long, or too nakedly, and she would start to wonder if he was really the entirely trustworthy guy he usually seemed to be.

When she glanced up from the laminated list of desserts, she said, "You know how when you get up in the middle of the night to pee and then when you come back to bed the guy you're with sort of half wakes up and makes room for you, or opens the covers or something? Sometimes I think the only time I really trust David is then . . . Do you think that's crazy?"

Laura, though trying to appear earnest and interested, was a little bit embarrassed by Annabeth's confession. "Well, physical intimacy is pretty important . . ." she said, and Annabeth nodded more vigorously than was called for.

"It must be an occupational hazard or something," she said, trying to rewind the conversation. "I mean, I look at everything too closely. I'm always wondering where I can lose a few frames, you know?" It was a stretch as a joke, but it covered the awkwardness of her last remark—at least she hoped it did. Laura had her her head tilted and a kind of indulgent, or maybe just condescending, look on her face.

In fact, Laura was wondering if she, herself, seemed like extraneous footage to Annabeth at that moment. Maybe she had been coming on a little strong? Why was she trying to sell this other woman so hard? It really shouldn't matter what Annabeth Jensen thought. Who was Annabeth Jensen anyway?

They paid the check and cut through the back of the café to the clothing store. Annabeth was almost completely absorbed in fantasies about the comments she might make about the script she had not yet read. She pictured herself getting to the heart of the matter—the problem would be something about Bunny, something the author couldn't see because she couldn't see herself and that Laura couldn't name because she was too focused on . . . well, something else.

Laura, meanwhile, had fallen under the spell of an artfully cut blue-black jacket. It said Dior "new look" to her but would work well with jeans. She called Annabeth over as she slipped it on in front of a nearby full-length mirror.

"Isn't this perfect?" she asked.

Annabeth had to agree that it was. She couldn't help wondering why she never spotted anything that suited her the way this jacket suited Laura. They were almost exactly the same size, after all, despite their differences in build and coloring.

"Should I get it?" Laura asked, pulling the price tag into view.

Annabeth's answer was hardly necessary, however, because Laura was already carrying the item up to the register, where there was a line. Annabeth looked at her watch and calculated the time remaining on her parking meter to be dangerously short. But it would be unfriendly to dash off just at that moment, so she followed her new friend to the cashier, where Laura was gazing at the array of credit cards in her wallet. She smiled at Annabeth and then made a mock frown.

"I can never decide which one to use," she said. "Do I want the mileage or the tax deduction?" Then, approaching the register, she withdrew what appeared to be a Corporate American Express card. Annabeth wondered if film directors were allowed to deduct a certain amount of their income for wardrobe purchases. It seemed highly unlikely. Especially fifteen-hundred-dollar jackets—for that was what the blazer cost. Annabeth had never spent that much on anything that wasn't a motor vehicle. Laura, she realized miserably, was not just beautiful and talented, she was rich.

But Laura was only acting with the eternal optimism of the hustling young director. She had no offer on the table that justified the purchase of a fifteen-hundred-dollar blazer—she hardly had a script. She had met with dozens of potential producers, including the suddenly elusive Simpson, but it was unclear now—after almost four years of schmoozing—if she could get *Trouble Doll* made at all. The producers were always at the wrong point in their production cycle, or not certain enough of the foreign markets, or felt that the script—any script—might not be adequately "castable." Laura kept these setbacks from derailing her by granting herself a "clean slate" every six months or so. She always said the script needed "one more draft" because there was no point in saying two, or three, or four more. The next "official" draft had to be good enough to submit to actors—that was all she knew. Laura was glad to have come across Annabeth, though. A smart editor was crucial. She had been sincere in her interview with the *Weekly* insofar as she thought cutting film was the best way on earth to learn how cinema works. She *would* cut all her own films, if she could be two places at once, but second best would be to have an editor who was smart, competent, and completely in her pocket, immune to the influence of studios, actors, awards ceremonies, et cetera. So if Annabeth's last picture—the title of which she kept forgetting, probably because Annabeth hadn't yet learned the trick of saying *Golden State* instead of "the feature I cut"—was any good at all, she was pretty sure she would hire her to cut *Trouble Doll*.

Annabeth's parking meter had expired when she finally got back to her Honda and there was a ticket for almost fifty bucks tucked under the wiper.

"It's weird," said Laura to Greg, a few days later. "I feel like I'm dating her."

"What's that supposed to mean?" Greg wasn't interested in his wife's latest lunch date—they all seemed the same after a while.

"Well, she's not really someone I need to cultivate professionally, and she can be a bit . . . snarky, but sometimes there's this, I don't know, momentum when we talk, like when you have a crush on someone in high school . . . It's just weird."

Greg nodded and looked at his coffee cup. He wished he had a job designing coffee cups. He'd make them gray-green and translucent, the color of seawater on a cloudy day.

"For a second there, I thought you were interested," said Laura.

"I have a short attention span," he said. He looked up at his wife, who was beautiful—even first thing in the morning, no makeup, scowling at him. It filled him with wonder for a split second, and then too quickly with resentment.

Laura didn't know what he was thinking, but her exquisitely sensitive appetite for flattery could slurp up even an infinitesimal flicker. "I realize this is magical thinking or whatever, but I feel like she was put in my path for a reason, like she has something to give me," she said.

"Like what?"

"Ideas, maybe. She's a real movie nerd," said Laura and then, after a pause: "She doesn't know how smart she is."

Greg's eyes were now tracking along the sports page, though he nodded and, noticing her pause, looked up to ask, "So are we going to Montecito this weekend?"

"Do you want to?"

"Not really," said Greg. "I need to spend some time in the studio," which was what he always said when he meant "I don't think

I can last that long without a jag." A jag was an anonymous sexual encounter, the pursuit of which was what kept his mind occupied for almost half his waking life. (The rest of the time he spent hating himself.)

Laura nodded and picked up her coffee cup to put it in the sink. She knew he wasn't doing much painting lately, but there was always the possibility that he'd start up again. The first time she'd seen his work, in a group show somewhere near the Bradbury building downtown, it had taken her breath away. The pictures were fluid and delicate-looking, rendered in what looked at first like pencil, but up close was revealed to be the artist's fingerprints. They were portraits of the faces of condemned men, but Laura had not recognized that at the time. Later, Greg had destroyed dozens of these drawings, saying they were cynical and gimmicky. He had then begun to make paintings that he sometimes said were about torture but were really only different-sized rectangles of uniformly applied, carefully blended paint: gray, red, and blue. They couldn't have been very much fun to make, and now he rarely made them anyway. His annual allowance paid their living expenses (just barely), so what was the point?

Part 2

CASTING

8

Whenever the phone rang during the early months of their acquaintance, Annabeth imagined that it was Laura calling to announce the commencement of her new life. She was not quite waiting by the phone, but she did hesitate to call Laura first, and when a few weeks went by with no word she felt disproportionately crushed, forgotten. Then, one Saturday morning, the phone rang and the voice on the other end *was* Laura's. Annabeth's fantasies were reanimated in seconds.

"Hey, I was having brunch down here at Hal's and I thought I could swing by and drop off a copy of the script on the way home," Laura said, as though three weeks of silence had not passed between them. "I've been having smoke blown up my ass by this Simpson guy and I need a reality check." She'd actually brought the script to give to the newly re-interested producer but, during the course of their brunch, she had decided to hold off. Once you give someone a mediocre script, you can't get it back. There was no danger of killing Annabeth's enthusiasm, though, and if Simpson could really get the thing to the people he claimed he could get it to, she wanted to make sure he got the version that would do the trick.

Annabeth read *Trouble Doll* twice that afternoon—and again the following morning. David read it on Sunday evening while Annabeth made dinner. In his eyes, it was a melodrama . . . *The Perils of Pauline,* except that in this version, Pauline cursed a lot, her boyfriend had tattoos, and the train finally ran her over after all.

"Am I crazy, or did that kind of suck?" David asked as he seated himself on their back steps with a beer. Annabeth was grilling tuna steaks.

The remark stopped Annabeth in her tracks. Her desire to have a job on Laura's movie and for that movie to start shooting sooner rather than later had enabled her to see an appealingly quirky coming-of-age story shimmering behind the melodrama.

"Well . . . I kind of liked Bunny."

"Really? Maybe I missed something. She seemed pretty lame to me."

"I think that might be the point."

"That she's lame?"

"That she doesn't make any real decisions about her life until it's too late."

David considered this statement. It certainly sounded like a movie plot, at least in terms of the brief summaries he was used to reading on the backs of video boxes and in the TV listings. On the other hand, it bore little resemblance to the script he had read. But this was Annabeth's area of expertise and he trusted that she knew more about it than he did—a little bit, anyway. Plus, she'd read the thing three times.

"So, what are you going to say to Laura?"

"I'm not sure. I thought I'd write up my notes, though. So she has something in her hand to refer to when she talks to the writer."

"So you're pretty sure you'll have at least a page worth of something to say?"

She paused, uncertain. "Well, if nothing else, I can point out which scenes I think are really carrying the story and make suggestions about how to consolidate some of the better character stuff into them."

"Like what? I mean, what did you think was good character stuff?"

"Well, like the way she makes sure to exchange all her tip money for larger bills—so she won't have to use the fives and ones those creeps handled to buy her groceries and put gas in her car."

"I wondered what that was about."

"Yeah. It would make more sense if you saw her doing it right after the scene in the strip club. Anyway, stuff like that."

David looked impressed, so Annabeth felt reassured and later that evening, she came up with more than two pages of additional suggestions. It was easy to see that the story's intended resolution (Bunny disappears, but since she's told everyone she's going home to Tulsa, no one in Los Angeles realizes that she's been killed) was kind of a cheat. It was hard to believe even stupid Bunny was stupid enough to double-cross Sasha, the club owner. The script ended with an homage to *All About Eve,* a bit wherein a new girl goes through the motions of Bunny's onstage routine, preparing to take her place. It was clever, but not at all satisfying emotionally. Annabeth felt the audience would spend the last minutes of the film wishing for more information about Bunny— who she was, why she acted the way she did. It wasn't the worst place to leave an audience, but not if you did so just because you couldn't figure out how to leave them with a sense of closure. Resolution, after all, is one thing that movies reliably do better than life.

She called Laura the next morning and left a message saying she had lots of notes, but after three days, Laura had still not called back. Annabeth began to brood. Did she really want notes, or just encouragement? In film school at U.T., Annabeth's classmates had tended to bristle and spit at anything she said that would have required them to rewrite or rethink. The only comments they seemed to find acceptable were quibbles about dialogue or the confusing use of a prop or some continuity issue, things that would easily be corrected *if you ever got to shoot the thing.* First you needed a story that could hold the audience's interest, not to mention one that made sense. Even in paraprofessional L.A., it often seemed that all writers really wanted to know when they gave her their scripts to read was "Do you love me?" Still, Laura had not written *Trouble Doll* and this Ramona person was nowhere in sight. In all likelihood, Laura really did want to make the script as good as possible, and thus maybe she really did want to hear Annabeth's thoughts on the subject.

Annabeth decided to start with the note that would be most flattering to Laura as the director: that the script needed to be more visual—to *show* the viewer who Bunny really is, how she lives, and the fantasy world of L.A. that seems just out of her reach. When she called Laura again, Laura picked up the phone, but on recognizing Annabeth's voice, the first thing she said was "Want to come with me to LACMA? They're showing that Stones movie *Cocksucker Blues*."

"Sure," said Annabeth. She loved going to the movies at the museum—their screening room was so much nicer than a regular movie theater and the audience so much more human than the people who showed up at industry screenings. She'd actually seen Robert Frank's documentary in Austin but she wouldn't mind seeing it again, especially with Laura. "Do you want me to bring my notes on *Trouble Doll*?" she asked.

In fact, since Saturday morning Laura had reread the draft herself and was no longer so sure she wanted to hear what Annabeth had to say. "You read it already?"

"Didn't you get my message?"

"The thing is, it's looking like Elisabeth Shue might really be interested, so we're probably going to have to do a whole new draft for *her,* but sure, bring your notes. The movie's at six-thirty. Meet me in the courtyard; I'll get the tickets." Elisabeth Shue? From *Adventures in Babysitting*? That was a "real" actress?

Annabeth arrived at the museum at five-thirty. There was some kind of event being set up with a stage and speakers, and trays of hors d'oeuvres were coming out of a catering trailer. A lot of rock 'n' roll types were milling around looking lost, kids with big hair and pegged jeans—they didn't know their way around the museum but had come to see the legendary documentary. An early sprinkling of people was also starting to arrive for the night's courtyard event, swing-dance enthusiasts. This group was for the most part younger than the rock 'n' roll crowd and wore their own very specific costumes. Finally, there were two minority factions: much older swing-dance fans, perhaps of the original vintage, and fortyish African-American jazz enthusiasts—the dance band featured a local keyboard player who was going to blow the roof off the roofless courtyard, and his friends and neighbors had come to cheer him on.

Annabeth circled and observed but could not find Laura. She was only a little anxious. It made a certain amount of sense that Laura would be late, although Annabeth was starting to doubt that there would be any tickets left for sale when she did arrive. Nevertheless, it was an interesting crowd and the experience of just being outside among other humans was so rare that she was enjoying herself thoroughly; it was like a wedding without any family. Soon they were going to start selling drinks, and Annabeth thought maybe it would be just as much fun to have a cocktail on the concrete plaza and listen to the swing band as to file into the auditorium with all those sallow rock 'n' roll fans. When she saw Laura sauntering toward her from the direction of the museum entrance, she was smiling a relaxed and happy smile, as though it had never occurred to her that there was any urgency about their situation. Annabeth waved; Laura shrugged. When she got within earshot, she explained the shrug:

"It's sold out, I'm sorry. It never occurred to me it would be such a scene."

"It's okay," Annabeth said, "I've been having a great time just watching the crowd."

Laura made a skeptical face and looked around. "Funny mix," she said. "When does the band start?"

"I don't know. Probably not till seven, right?"

"Well, let's go upstairs and see some art, and then we can come down and have a drink."

It had not occurred to Annabeth to enter the museum. She hoped Laura wouldn't be the sort of person who wanted to have long, analytical conversations about the artwork within earshot of other patrons.

"You're shivering," said Laura. "Are you cold?"

"A little, I guess."

"Here," said Laura, removing her blazer and handing it to Annabeth—it was the one she'd bought at American Rag. When Annabeth put it on, the silky lining was warm and smelled like Laura. The jacket felt light on her shoulders and fit beautifully, skimming her wrist and hip bones, tapering at her waist. Despite the T-shirt and Levi's she had on underneath, she felt suddenly sleek and well put together.

She followed Laura upstairs to a gallery where work by a photographer named Lewis Baltz was on display. The photos were eerie, mostly barren industrial landscapes, piles of trash, ruined interiors. Annabeth found them compelling but had no idea why. Laura hated them because, she said, they "looked smug." Annabeth nodded, trying to imagine what Laura meant, but all she could think about was how smug she, herself, felt in Laura's blazer.

"Hey," said Laura, "let's dance!"

"What?"

"Downstairs." The band had started playing. "C'mon, it'll be fun."

"I don't know how," said Annabeth.

"I'll teach you," said Laura, heading across the gallery toward the exit.

Annabeth didn't follow. She had been poleaxed by the sight of her own Doc Marten–clad feet; they might as well have been lead-soled. She saw herself attempting to dance, staggering like Frankenstein's monster, tripping and stumbling, then reaching for support as Laura's fifteen-hundred-dollar blazer sheared open at the shoulder, ruined, beyond repair.

Laura turned to see why Annabeth's footsteps had not followed her own. "Don't be ridiculous," she said, reading Annabeth's apparent terror. "It'll be fun. Just watch."

Annabeth stepped closer while Laura lifted her arms slightly to provide an unobstructed view of her feet. "It's just one, two, three-and one, two, three-and one," she explained as her feet performed a slow-motion swing step.

Annabeth followed tentatively, making no obvious mistakes but knowing that skills performed flawlessly during the instruction phase were no proof against disaster on the dance floor.

Down in the courtyard, Laura backed her way in among the dancers, beckoning Annabeth forward. But after a few agonized strides, Annabeth shook her head no and began to retreat. Laura made a pleading look, then slipped her glance outward, and, as though summoned, a tall black man stepped forward and offered her his hand. Laura looked at Annabeth for her approval, Annabeth nodded, and the two were off.

Taking a seat at a nearby table, Annabeth relaxed at last. The band was swinging, Laura was obviously having a great time, and Annabeth was wearing the coolest blazer on earth. She wondered whether David would like this scene, and if he knew how to dance. She couldn't picture it, but then again, she wouldn't have been able to picture Laura dancing either, and there she was, sassily waving her hand beside her face in time with her feet like she'd been doing it all her life.

After another number, Laura returned to Annabeth's little café table and sat down.

"You're a really good dancer," said Annabeth.

"You're a really good wallflower," said Laura.

"Yeah, well. Lots of practice. Plus, I enjoy it . . ."

"Well, there you go." Laura looked around, craning her neck to take in the whole scene.

"Do you want your blazer?" said Annabeth.

"I'm all sweaty," said Laura, making a face.

"You might catch cold. Sorry, I seem to be channeling someone's mom."

"Not yours?"

"No, not mine."

"Where's your car?" asked Laura.

"Over on Spaulding."

"Mine's in front of the Tar Pits. Walk me and then I'll drive you over."

"Sure," said Annabeth, though it hadn't been a question.

——

The La Brea Tar Pits are contained in a parklike enclosure in an otherwise entirely urban part of Los Angeles. Driving by, one sees only a lagoon overhung by ferny trees. In the burbling shallows of that lagoon, however, are a group of monumental bronze sculptures: a family of woolly mammoths, one of them trapped in the tar and trumpeting desperately in the direction of her small child on the opposite shore. The baby mammoth's trunk is extended toward the mother in reply. As Laura and Annabeth strolled by the lagoon, the sulfur smell caused Annabeth to look closely at this scene for the first time. Unprepared for its narrative force, she felt her eyes well up with tears. Mother stuff always got to her. Embarrassed, she began rooting around in her pockets for a tissue, forgetting until she felt the silk lining that the jacket she was wearing belonged to Laura.

"What are you looking for?" asked Laura.

"Nothing," said Annabeth.

"Gum?" asked Laura. "I have some Altoids in the car."

"It's those fucking woolly mammoths," said Annabeth. "I've never really looked at them before."

Laura followed the direction of Annabeth's derisive nod. "I wonder how many millions of dollars *that* cost," she said.

"Prehistoric kitsch," Annabeth muttered.

"They should put that on the state flag instead of the whaddayacallit," said Laura.

"Bruin?" asked Annabeth.

By then they had arrived at Laura's car, a beautifully preserved black Karmann Ghia. Annabeth was fascinated by its smell—the leather upholstery was too old to offer much odor but when combined with the smells of motor oil, old machinery, Laura's perfume, and Altoids, it was an evocative mix. As Laura buckled herself in and started the engine, Annabeth realized she was still wearing the wildly expensive blazer and began to take it off before fastening her own seat belt. She didn't want it to get wrinkled.

"You should keep it," said Laura, recognizing what Annabeth was trying to do. "I didn't realize it read so blue. It's much better on you than on me—brings out your eyes."

Annabeth didn't know what to say, and by the time she coughed up the words "But it looks great on you," they no longer sounded like part of the same conversation.

"Where'd you say you were parked?" said Laura.

"Over there—make a right at the light."

Annabeth stared blankly through the windshield, trying to decide whether to go on resisting Laura's gift. She hadn't even seen how the jacket looked on her; she only knew how it felt.

As they turned the corner onto Spalding, Annabeth realized she hadn't even mentioned the script. It was still in the back seat of her car, which they were fast approaching. "I really loved *Trouble Doll*," she said. And she *had* loved it, in spite of seeing its deficiencies . . . but most of all she had loved it because it was the project she was going to work on with Laura, the one that would make all this discomfort and maneuvering worthwhile. They would become real partners, like Martin Scorsese and Thelma Schoonmaker or Arthur Penn and Dede Allen.

"Thanks," said Laura. "She's still a little fuzzy, Bunny, but I think the opening sequence helps with that, don't you?"

"When she's watching the other girl at the club?"

"No, the very beginning, walking down the highway."

"Oh, yeah," said Annabeth. "Do you want the script back? It's in my car. I made some notes—"

"No, that's okay," said Laura. "We can talk about it more when we really get going. Anyway, tonight was fun." Simpson had ultimately talked her into giving the current draft to Elisabeth Shue. And if it *wasn't* really ready, she didn't want to know.

"Yeah, really fun! Thanks."

"Don't thank me."

"For the blazer."

"Okay, you can thank me for that. Call me, okay?"

Annabeth got into her own car and took a deep whiff for comparison. It smelled like a car, nothing more, nothing less. The blazer, however, still smelled like Laura. She hung it up carefully when she got home, even though opening the closet door made a creaking sound and David was asleep on the couch.

The next morning, she saw that her priorities had gotten confused, and as soon as the hour seemed reasonable enough, she drove to Laura's house (the address was on the script) to deliver her notes and, reluctantly, offer Laura back her blazer. Greg answered the door, looking like he'd just gotten out of bed. He was wearing nothing but a much-laundered pair of gray sweatpants and Annabeth couldn't help but notice, even with her eyes trained only on his face, that his genitals were distinctly outlined by the clinging fabric.

"Annabeth-the-editor?" he said, after looking at her briefly, and then, "Come in. The coffee's just about to spurt." He seemed friendly enough but, sensing that Laura might not actually be home, she hesitated. Greg was very handsome in a Waspy, dissolute way—as long as she kept her eyes above his waist. As if reading her mind he said, "Sorry you caught me *en déshabillé*, so to speak."

"I'm late for an appointment," she lied, improvising. She took the script out of the shopping bag that also held the jacket, carefully turned inside out and folded. Obviously, Greg would have accepted both items without argument.

"Ah, your notes," he said. "She's at the gym, I guess."

"Nice to meet you," said Annabeth.

"My pleasure," said Greg, shaking the hair off his forehead and looking over her shoulder. And then, sure enough, she did hear a spurting sound coming from inside.

"My fix," said Greg, "if you will. Gotta go."

And Annabeth nodded, relieved to be left alone on the doorstep, her mission accomplished, and the blazer still in hand.

Two weeks later, Laura and Greg drove into the desert to attend a party at a friend's bungalow near Joshua Tree. It made Laura a little bit uncomfortable to leave town with *Trouble Doll* now hovering so close to a deal. Simpson had heard from his contact at UTA that Elisabeth Shue had been "adoring" the script, which she was halfway through. An official response was due at any moment, and in Laura's mind scouting, casting, and the hiring of department heads was all but finished. As they made their way through the endless fields of metal windmills, she decided on a DP, a production designer, a first assistant director, and an editor—more or less.

"So what did you think of young Annabeth, anyway?" she asked Greg.

"Cute," said Greg.

"Did she seem smart to you?"

"I met her for thirty seconds, Laura." But his wife often sought his advice on subjects like this—people he barely knew, books he hadn't read, scenes she hadn't shot yet.

"I think she's more ambitious than she lets on."

"Is that a bad thing?" Greg asked.

"I mean, what if she actually just likes to cut film?"

She considered this possibility while checking her reflection in the visor-mounted vanity mirror. Maybe the shamefully expensive face cream worked. "I'm sure she does," she said. It was Annabeth's unwillingness to just come out and say what she presumably wanted—to cut *Trouble Doll*—that made Laura uncomfortable. Growing up, she'd had a cat named Herman Munster who used to bring mauled birds to Laura's bedside and then sit waiting for her to wake up. She had scolded him and put him outdoors every time it happened, but he never seemed to catch on that she didn't want the dead birds. Annabeth was like Herman Munster, somehow.

"Are they going to be playing tonight, do you think?" Greg asked, meaning the members of the band who were throwing the party.

She knew he was insecure among this crowd—Art Center graduates who had known him when he was actually showing and selling work, and when that work was actually good. It surprised her that he had even agreed to go to the party. She was starting to see Joshua trees on the side of the road, which meant they were getting close to their destination. "I think they just want to kick back," she answered.

———

After a few tequila shots, Laura hit the dance floor. She was a fabulous, if narcissistic, dancer and could go on for hours, no partner necessary. Throughout the party, she played a game with herself where she had to make eye contact with as many men as she could without any of them successfully engaging her in conversation. One guy tried to grab her on her way to the bathroom, but she stopped him with a look. Greg sat outside in the dark, smoking pot with their host's teenage son and his friends, who told him about their bungee-jumping adventures at the Devil's Punchbowl.

On the way home, after forty-five minutes of silence, Greg said, "Why did you act like such a twat tonight?"

"Because I can't stand being married to a zombie," Laura said.

"Bullshit. You just needed to charge your batteries. And I'm the idiot who chauffeured you into the desert for two hours so you could shake your ass in Mike Viola's face."

Eventually they were both so mad they had to pull over. When the car was stationary, they stalked off on separate tangents into the black nothingness: Laura kept to the asphalt, Greg scrabbled into the dry vegetation, where the tip of his cigarette glowed as he drew on it. It was the only thing Laura could see. She was afraid of snakes, scorpions, and large spiders, all of which could easily have been slithering around in the creosote. After a while, she realized he probably couldn't see her at all, so she returned to the car and sat in the passenger seat with the door open. She missed the days when her husband had been faithful to her, when he never came home at five in the morning still revved on coke, but she could not bring herself to ask him what had happened because she was afraid of how she, herself, might figure in his answer.

Greg finally sauntered back, pulled her around to his side of the car, and told her to get on her knees, which she did. "I'm going to trust you not to hurt me," he said, but when she nodded he held her chin. "And not to do anything but exactly what I tell you." And so, crouching while Greg sat halfway inside the car, she blew him. Two cars passed but didn't slow—Laura pictured Greg's stoned, shut-down face captured momentarily in their headlights.

9

"How much have I told you about Simpson?" Laura asked Annabeth one morning on the phone.

"Not much."

"Well, now that we're actually working together, I've been hearing some weird things about him."

Annabeth wasn't sure why Laura was telling her this. "Really?" she asked.

"Like, he says he's just back from a few years in London, which is true because I checked around. But I got a couple of different versions of why he left. Everyone agrees there was some kind of a problem with an ex-girlfriend, a model. My friend Cass said he'd threatened the girl with a gun when she broke up with him. And Becca Lawson heard he was stalking her, and she got him deported or something. And we're talking about a guy who looks like Opie."

"But still, nothing that disqualifies him from being a good producer."

"Well, he's been getting the script to the right people—that's all I care about. I wasn't sure it was ready to go out to actors, but he writes these incredible ass-kissing, name-dropping cover letters. 'The role of Bunny combines the toughness of Streep's Sophie with the vulnerability of Monroe in *Some Like It Hot.*' Shit like that."

"Wow," said Annabeth. "What happened to Elisabeth Shue?"

"Oh, she was never right for it," said Laura, and then listed all the actresses they were now considering, as well as some character actors to play the part of the Sasha, the club owner. "Simpson reminds me a little bit of my liar, but I guess that's inevitable," said Laura, rerouting Annabeth's train of thought.

"Your liar?"

"This guy I used to work for, Jon Golden."

Annabeth knew the name—he was a producer of some renown. "I didn't know you worked for him."

"Yeah, for almost two years. I was, like, twenty-two. Some months I got paid, other months, no such luck."

"Is that why you call him 'my liar'?" asked Annabeth.

"That and everything else. He lied about every deal he ever made: how much the budget was, who'd agreed to be in it, when it would start . . . he made his living by lying."

"You called him that to his face?"

"Oh, totally. He thought it was hilarious."

"And Simpson reminds you of him? That doesn't sound good."

"Well, it is what it is. He's a producer," said Laura. And then she remembered to ask Annabeth if she could pick up their mail and water their plants while they were in Santa Barbara over Thanksgiving.

The interior of Laura and Greg's house didn't quite correspond to its Spanish exterior and Old Hollywood location in Annabeth's eyes, but the general tenor of the decor made sense for Laura: spare, clean, modern. Watering the plants took five minutes so, afterward, she sat on the leather couch and leafed through a copy of *Vanity Fair,* sat at the dining table and tried to forget the Bronsteins' Thanksgiving dinner the night before, stood at the back door and wondered how much Laura and Greg paid the gardener to trim the impossibly steep but grassy lawn, and, finally, made her way upstairs. There was no reason for her to do so—no plants up there she'd been told to tend to, and she was not entirely comfortable about entering the private precincts of Laura's domain— but the ride home was so long, it seemed reasonable to wait until the sun would no longer be directly in her eyes while driving.

It had really been too soon for Annabeth to spend Thanksgiving with David's family. Seeing him surrounded by people who had known him since childhood, she discovered that she was woefully ignorant about his past. For one thing, he'd apparently gone through a major ceramics phase in college—the house was full of bowls, plates, and mugs he had "thrown" himself. This information just plain gave her the creeps. She also found out that, until very recently, David, his sister, his parents, his father's two brothers, and their families had spent two weeks skiing up at Mammoth every winter, where they owned a condo. When she'd asked him why he'd stopped going, he'd said he hadn't been able to get the time off from the library. She could tell he was lying, but not why or how much. She'd ultimately gotten through the evening by drinking a great deal and attaching herself to David's sister's loserish single friend, a woman named Mona who did something administrative at the L.A. Philharmonic. But even Mona didn't seem very interested in Annabeth's work. And without that as a conversational fallback, Annabeth had started to feel pretty loserish herself. Everyone the Bronsteins knew seemed to be a brainiac of some kind (law professor, research scientist), or at any rate they all had professions that required advanced degrees: David's sister was an architect, and her husband a gastroenterologist. It was uncanny to find two dozen people who lived in Los Angeles and had no interest in the movie business, but there they were.

In Laura's bedroom, Annabeth opened the his and hers side-by-side closets. This wasn't really snooping because, she told herself, her intent was not prurient. What sex toys they might own or whether or not Laura padded her bra were not the information she was after, and she already knew what Laura's wardrobe looked like. The closets contained shirts, pants, and a smattering of dressier pieces hung on neatly spaced hangers—some in garment bags. T-shirts, jeans, and sweaters in a very limited palette (gray, black, white, occasionally olive green or navy blue) were folded and piled neatly on open shelves. They must spend almost as much on dry cleaning as she did on rent, Annabeth calculated. What did it cost to live like this? Greg was from what she presumed was a wealthy family back East (how else could he afford to be a painter?). She knew he had gone to a fancy New York prep school, anyway. But she knew very little about Laura's family. The night tables and bookshelves offered a surprising dearth of mementos—no framed photos, no collections or keepsakes—and even the bedside books seemed neutral. On what seemed to be Greg's side of the bed there was a book of essays by the neurologist Oliver Sacks; on Laura's, a Dorothy Sayers novel. Both seemed equally unlikely to have been read.

Stymied in her effort to find any clues to the inner Laura but not yet ready to leave, Annabeth decided to take a shower in the extraordinary glass box she had spotted in the master bath. Its six fierce nozzles sprayed her head, chest, and hips, and once wet she helped herself to the extraordinarily silky French shower gel and salon-only brand of shampoo. She even picked up and examined the pumice stone, although she wasn't entirely sure what to do with the thing. Upon turning off the Hydra-headed shower, however, Annabeth encountered an unforeseen problem: how to dry herself without leaving behind evidence in the form of a used towel. She stood dripping in the stall for almost a minute while she mentally composed elements of a plausible explanation—she'd been stuck in traffic, the AC in her car had died, she was on her way out to dinner from Laura's. (As though Laura would have begrudged her a few tablespoonfuls of bath products and the five cents' worth of laundry detergent it would cost to remove Annabeth's cooties from one of a dozen pima cotton bath sheets! But Annabeth's sense of having transgressed was stronger than any logic.)

Ultimately, she decided to air-dry by walking naked around the master suite. The afternoon sun was hot enough to make quick work of this. In passing, she saw herself in the mirror on the closet door—a bright lozenge of sunlight made her white skin luminous next to the chocolate brown of the bedroom walls. She turned her back and cast a look over her shoulder at her reflected image. The sight made her feel sexy and strong. For a few seconds, she even lay down on the king-sized bed, picturing the white bedspread's raised pattern becoming imprinted on her back and thighs. She was tempted to masturbate but didn't dare. Getting up to dress, she caught a faint trace of Laura's perfume. She'd never gotten around to asking what it was called. Now she could find out for herself.

Returning to the bathroom, she looked for a supplementary medicine cabinet—she had already found the one over the sink to contain only dental floss, aspirin, and similar essentials. Where were the prescription meds, the tampons, the beauty secrets? At last, she realized that the full-length mirror in the bathroom was, in fact, a spring-loaded door. The cabinet behind it was also full-length—it contained an astounding trove of products; here was the mother lode.

The shelves at eye level appeared to hold the bulk of Laura's frequently used cosmetics. There was a jar of the five-hundred-dollar face cream Annabeth had read about in a magazine at the dentist's office. Beside that was a fluted glass flacon of Laura's perfume, a brand Annabeth had never seen before, French. She'd lifted the bottle to smell the nozzle—she hadn't yet even decided to try a spritz—when the sound of the mail falling through the slot downstairs startled her and she dropped the tiny bottle on the bathroom's stone floor, where it shattered.

She gazed in frozen terror at the mess of broken glass and amber liquid as the smell of orange blossoms, sandalwood, and something else—cork?—overtook the room. There were tiny shards of glass glittering across the tops of her pale bare feet. Ultimately, she was forced to use one of the fancy towels to make a walkway for herself, which meant she had to do a load of laundry in addition to cleaning up the mess, and then drive to Beverly Hills to find more of the mysterious perfume. Barneys, the third store she visited, was the only one that carried it. By the time she'd acquired the replacement bottle (for eighty-five dollars, not counting all that valet parking at the stores!) she felt exhausted almost to the point of tears. Then, back in Laura's bathroom, she realized that to complete the illusion she would have to empty the atomizer to the previous level. She sprayed a fair amount of fragrance into the backyard, but at a certain point she had to admit defeat and leave the too-full bottle where she had found its predecessor so many hours before.

Asleep in her Venice bedroom that night, Annabeth had another version of her elephant-and-sewing-machine dream. This time, she was wearing the elephant hide and the sewing machine was running on its own, furiously. She woke up terrified that it would sew her. The dreamed machine was not the beige Pfaff she'd grown up with; it had a distinctive matte green finish, like an old Burroughs adding machine.

"A Singer?" David asked her, stroking her hair. "A siren, sucking you in?"

"I don't think so." Annabeth wondered if her dream could possibly be that cleverly encoded. She doubted it. "My dreams aren't that literary."

"It's not literary, it's just how they work sometimes. Haven't you ever had one like that? Where it all turned out to be an anagram or something?"

"No, have you?"

"I used to have one about a bee that was gathering cocaine instead of pollen. It drove me crazy for months. Then one day I realized that cocaine with a B was Cobain."

"So what did that mean?"

He looked sheepish for a moment, and Annabeth decided not to press him.

"Well, my elephant hide isn't an anagram, I know that much."

What is *it hiding then?* David wanted to ask, but Annabeth obviously wasn't interested in wordplay. And that was terribly disappointing.

10

Annabeth wore Laura's blazer the night they met for dinner at Kate Mantilini. It was dressier than her usual attire, but by wearing it she felt she was somehow protecting herself from inquiries about the missing/replaced bottle of fragrance. Remember, it said, you trust me, you like me, you even gave me this jacket.

Laura had come straight from an advance screening of *Interview with the Vampire,* and the first thing she said was "If anyone ever talks me into casting Tom Cruise, shoot me in the heart with a silver bullet." It was a line she'd been working on the whole way over, but her offhand delivery convinced Annabeth that it was a spontaneous quip. Annabeth had not seen the movie, but she didn't question that a day would come when Laura Katz would be in a position to say no to one of the two or three most powerful actors in Hollywood. When they were seated Annabeth asked how Laura's Thanksgiving had been.

"Oh, God, didn't I tell you?" said Laura, which of course she hadn't. "It was hellish! My mother booked us all into this little inn up in a canyon that was supposedly haunted, or holy, or some shit. The woman at the desk was, like, *The whole compound was sacred to the Chumash.*" Laura paused and smiled to herself. "Remember *It's not nice to fool Mother Nature?*"

Annabeth didn't remember, but she smiled in an ambiguous way, just to keep Laura talking. She had never heard Laura mention a mother before and had for some reason assumed that her parents were dead.

"Anyway, our room smelled like a dead animal, there were doilies every six inches, and Greg got cramps from the organic vegetarian slop they served us for dinner. We left at two A.M. and checked into the Biltmore. We were very proud of ourselves."

"You had Thanksgiving dinner at the hippie place?"

"No, at my uncle's house in Montecito. Anyway, when I got back here I looked up those Chumash Indians, and guess what? They were bloodthirsty marauders. They'd practically extinguished *themselves* by the time Junípero Serra got there."

Laura pronounced the Franciscan monk's name in an elaborate, trilled, and whispered Spanish that implied mastery of the language. Annabeth worried that she wouldn't have begun to know where to "look up" the Chumash Indians. She didn't even know in what century Junípero Serra had "got there." If she did wind up working on *Trouble Doll,* Laura would expect her to know all these things that she didn't. She drank her second martini much too quickly.

When the entrées were served, Laura changed the subject. "So, I know why I don't usually go home for the holidays," she said to Annabeth. "What's your excuse?"

"Well, you know, it's a long haul to a cold place . . ."

"And?"

"And there's not much I would really call 'home' back in Duluth."

"Your parents are divorced?"

It was not the kind of question Annabeth had expected to answer, although she was flattered by Laura's interest. "Sort of," she said.

"Sort of?"

And so she told Laura some more—quite a bit more, as it turned out. She was drunk. She wrote down as much as she could remember when she got home because after dinner, while they were standing on Wilshire Boulevard waiting for the valets to return with their cars, Laura had asked Annabeth a funny question: "Hey, can I use any of that stuff?"

"What stuff?" said Annabeth, which seemed slightly friendlier than "What do you mean, *use*?"

"Well, like the thing about the basement might work in that scene where—well, no, you haven't read the new pages—"

"You mean in *Trouble Doll*?" Annabeth felt a charge—fear?

Laura smiled and shrugged vaguely, meaning "So can I?" or maybe "Where's the harm?" Then she looked out into the street for the valet and, after another moment, back at Annabeth. "Never mind. You're obviously not comfortable."

"It's just . . . I don't know," Annabeth began.

"That jacket looks great on you, by the way," said Laura, but the way she said it sounded as though maybe it didn't—or that Laura wanted her to wonder if it didn't. Was she supposed to offer to give it back now?

David was at KCRW when she got home that night and Annabeth was glad to be alone. She got out the spiral notebook where she sometimes recorded her dreams and wrote:

When I was about ten, I started reading Nancy Drew books and pretending I was a detective. There were two games I made up. In one, I would hide "clues" that I could put together into some kind of story. Stupid stuff could be clues: a bottle cap, a sock, a pencil—the point was that they were hidden and then the game was to explain why. Did a man in too much of a hurry to put on his second sock stop here? Did he hide the pencil in the fear that later it would be found and dusted for fingerprints?

My other game was looking for the secret staircases in our house. It was old and there were always noises that I couldn't explain, so I decided there had to be some hidden passageways. In retrospect, I was looking for a secret hiding place for myself, I think: where I could play without Jeff making fun of me, or hide when Mom and Dad were fighting. (Did I really once hear her call him a fag? That's what I told Laura. I can't imagine that word coming out of her mouth, but I also kind of remember it.) Anyway, eventually I found my spot—it wasn't actually hidden; it was just the alcove in the basement that was out of sight of the stairs. I should have realized it wasn't exactly a secret because there was a cot there, and a little radio, and a lamp. I guess it was where my dad had to sleep when he was on the outs with my mother.

After I first "found" the place (it had been there all along, of course, but at some point I guess I decided to make it A Discovery), I planted some clues, and then I didn't go back for a while. I was going to wait long enough so that I would forget about my last visit and discover the clues anew. And maybe the weather got nice enough to play outside. Anyway, one afternoon I finally went back down there and at first I thought the radio was on, because I thought I heard a voice. I decided that Russian spies were listening for coded transmissions from Moscow. But when I got to the place in the shelves where I could spy through them, I saw my brother jerking off. I'd never seen an erect penis before and I'd certainly never seen that haunted and slightly maniacal expression on Jeff's face. He was about fifteen, I guess.

Eventually I must have managed to forget about that—or maybe I was old enough to also be curious about getting another look, or maybe no time passed and I went back the next day. I remember rain, or maybe even sleet—I could hear it on the metal cellar doors—and I went to the alcove and turned on the little lamp and the radio and began to set up shop on the bed. Who knows what was I going to do? Maybe just read my latest Nancy Drew. But as I sat there I noticed a nasty smell and, sleuth that I was, started to look for its source. It didn't take long. There was a dead raccoon in the far corner, near the water heater.

Again, I didn't tell anyone, but I couldn't stop thinking about how the raccoon had gotten there, how it must have been trapped and no one heard it and it starved to death right there in our basement. As though a raccoon would not be able to get out the same way it got in, and—I now realize—as though a creature could starve to death in that house, whimper and cry and scratch and thrash, and no one would ever know. When I finally went back to the basement room again, everything was different. The mattress was folded in half on the cot. It looked so final. Like an army cot after the soldier is killed. That was the thing that ended the game for me. It seemed like a place where I might disappear, too.

11

In December, Nancy Travis turned down *Trouble Doll* in order to do *Fluke,* a talking-dog picture with Samuel Jackson and Matthew Modine. "Laura's someone I'd really like to work with," she told Simpson. "I adored *Two Chevrolets.*" (People loved to say how much they liked Laura's first film because it was virtually impossible to see—Disney had objected to the seven-second use of the song "Someday My Prince Will Come" to imply a character's sexual dysfunction and embargoed the film. If you had seen it, you had either been at Sundance in 1991 or knew someone who had a videotape.) In any case, this was bad news for Simpson's cast-Bunny-first strategy. They needed an actress who was indie enough for Laura to respect, commercial enough for her name to mean something to foreign distributors, and plausible as a skanky stripper with big dreams. Travis was the end of their list.

So Simpson implemented his Plan B: attach a cluster of quirky characters for the smaller, cameo parts—the *Reservoir Dogs* strategy, he called it. It would be a lot easier to get someone with a recognizable name to commit to an oddball script for a few days of work than getting some would-be ingenue to stake three months of her life on it. He hired a location scout and started telling people they were going to go at the first of the year. He figured they could shoot exteriors and ready-made locations while they dressed the strip club, where almost a third of the story took place. He also told Laura they needed Ramona to punch up Bunny's character, again.

Laura and Ramona had become friends at AFI almost ten years earlier. The two black-clad women had recognized each other instantly as necessary allies, unafraid to use the word *cunt* and able to keep up with their male classmates shot for shot at the bar, the pool table, and behind the camera. But after their fellowship year, when Laura optioned Ramona's script, their friendship began to fray. Laura felt she had overpaid, Ramona felt Laura was getting more than her money's worth. Then Laura vanished entirely to work on *Two Chevrolets*—for what turned out to be almost five years. When she reappeared, she was married to Greg, living in Hollywood, and acting like she was doing Ramona a big favor by renewing her long-lapsed option for five grand. Since then, things between them had been tense. It wasn't easy for Ramona to get herself over to Laura's house for rewrites just because some producer she'd never heard of thought he could sell the thing, but she went.

"Do you know *Fat City*?" Laura asked as the two women sat ignoring the plate of cookies that Laura had placed on the coffee table between them. "That's the feeling I want."

"Utter despair?" Ramona knew the movie, but she did not particularly admire it.

"Oh, come on, there's plenty of hope in that movie," said Laura, although Ramona's disdain was already causing her to question the truth of this assertion. "Well, *hope* is the wrong word. But I'm thinking about Susan Tyrrell's character. Bunny could be like a version of her before she hits the skids."

"Bunny isn't depraved, she's tragic," said Ramona, who was looking down at a torn cuticle she was in the process of stripping till it bled.

Laura knew enough not to continue with the *Fat City* analogy. It was just that analogies were the only way she knew to think about character. All she could do was try to come up with a better example while Ramona fidgeted. Most of her favorite pictures— *Chinatown, Badlands, The Graduate*—were too ironic, too detached. She wanted *Trouble Doll* to be more sincere, more like *Cutter's Way*, if she remembered it right.

"I have an idea," said Ramona, finally looking up at Laura. "Let's give her a scene with a kid in it. Like, a little girl who might one day grow up to be Bunny, if she's not careful." Laura considered this. "A tough little girl, like Jodie Foster in *Alice Doesn't Live Here Anymore*," Ramona continued.

Laura was nodding and had picked up a pad to write on. "So,

where? At night, right? So there's, like, an implied threat because the kid seems to be alone when Bunny finds her. What is she, eight? Nine?"

"How about in the supermarket?" said Ramona.

Laura loved this idea. It brought in a whole implied sociopolitical analysis. Of course, there was always the problem of turning around all the brand labels. But they could just shoot in tight. She started narrating for Ramona:

"We see Bunny in, let's say, the canned goods aisle. And her eye is drawn to something on the floor: a child's plastic barrette. The kind with those molded flowers on it. Blue or purple."

Ramona picked up the thread: "And then she sees the kid, who's farther down, staring at the soup cans. And Bunny goes up to her to give her back the barrette but the kid asks for her help. She wants to make tuna casserole. Bunny asks if she's done it before and who's going to eat it and tries to help her find the recipe on a soup can and, I don't know, does she fail or succeed?"

"Neither," said Laura. "The kid hears her older brother calling her name and runs off, scared."

"And so then, later, we can get some mileage out of Bunny finding the barrette again in her coat pocket! This is great!" Laura saw a strange shift of expression on Ramona's face. Greg had just walked into the room.

"I'm making coffee," he said. "Do you guys want some?" Catching the black-haired woman's eye, he'd felt a jolt of fear and excitement. Then he'd realized he hadn't fucked her, just sat across from her several times at his SA meeting in Burbank. He had no idea what, if anything, he had shared about in her presence, but he assumed that she knew at least the general outline.

He probably knew equally damning things about the anorexic-looking woman on the couch if he could remember any, but he couldn't.

"None for me," Ramona said.

"No, thanks, honey," said Laura, turning to smile more intimately than was usual and to check on her husband's face. She could tell that he and Ramona had met before but decided, ultimately, that Ramona wasn't Greg's type. Too Goth-looking, and basically just not "cute." Laura felt she would know in her bones if she crossed paths with anyone who was a real threat and, in the absence of those crossings, the idea of the occasional also- or almost-ran in Greg's life was part of what kept her harness tight. His predatory gleam was a reason to keep her own hips slim, her skin firm, her hair glossy and kempt.

"Now, where were we?" she said to Ramona. "Right. The barrette."

12

Very early on the morning of January 17, David was standing in the kitchen when he heard the barking of dogs—it seemed to him later that he must have been troubled by the same things the dogs heard, because he'd woken up anxious and disoriented when the world outside was still silent.

When Annabeth opened her eyes the clock said it was four-thirty and she was alone in their bed, which was shaking like the little girl's bed in *The Exorcist*—erratically, violently. She became aware of the window over her head, which usually did such a pleasant job of waking her up when the sun came up over the fence, and she understood that the window was now a guillotine. The shaking stopped, but strange electric sounds continued to shear the darkness, sometimes accompanied by blue flashes. She found that she couldn't move; she couldn't think of where it might be safe to move. The door frame, a mere three strides away from the foot of the bed, seemed impossibly distant. The transformers blew, the dogs barked, the car alarms keened, and she was immobile.

"David?" she finally croaked, her voice sounding more peremptory than terrified.

"I'm out here. Are you okay?"

"Where?"

"In the kitchen. There's broken glass all over the place."

"Come back to bed."

It sounded like an invitation to sex. Her tone of voice had become utterly unpredictable.

"I'm barefoot," said David.

Annabeth's brain began to pace: the electricity was obviously out and would be for some time, and that triggered memories of the riots, not even two years ago. Nothing bad had befallen her then—she'd essentially watched it all on TV. She'd even gone out on a cleanup crew the following morning but, in the weeks that followed, she had become almost pathologically afraid of black people and their anger. There was something about the rage she'd seen that night that she recognized. On the morning of the Northridge quake, she felt that their cute little bungalow on the groovy southern edge of Venice was now far too close to Oakwood for her comfort. Maybe they could go to Laura's place—but then again, Laura's house was more or less straight up Western Avenue from South Central. Would there be roadblocks like before? Maybe it would be a better bet to head for David's parents' place in Mandeville Canyon. Would there be fires? How much cash did they have? How much gas was in the car?

David appeared in the bedroom doorway with a quart of milk in his hand, which he'd been drinking out of when the shaking started. He'd had the good sense to shut the fridge and then thought better of opening it again to replace the milk when the earthquake seemed over. He didn't realize he was still carrying the carton. In the shadows, he saw that Annabeth was curled up in a fetal position at the foot of the bed.

"I think I may have cut a tendon," he told Annabeth. "I'm bleeding. Can you help me?"

She watched him sit down uncertainly beside her, cradling his foot and applying pressure with the corner of the sheet. It was still dark in the room, but the soft white sheet was highly absorbent and the bloom of blood frightened her. She put her feet into his nearby flip-flops and scuttled to the bathroom. She thought twice about opening the hot-water tap, though she couldn't figure out why. Would it dispense snakes and spiders, like the girl's mouth in the fairy tale? Her thinking was definitely distorted. Was there a gas line open that had poisoned her?

She returned to the bedside and cleaned and bandaged David's foot by candlelight. His tendon was not torn. After she finished, they lay awake, waiting. She found that there was something oddly soothing about the idea that this was, at last, the Big One. Not so much because she had been living in fear of it—she hadn't. They had no emergency kit of canned goods and bottled water on hand. It was more a sense of closure, of justice having been done. The Los Angeles in which she lived, with its fragrant night air, its hallucinatory jacaranda blossoms, its gleaming ocean, and its idiotic surplus of wealth, deserved a setback. They all knew that, didn't they?

David was singing to himself softly, something about being sucked into a tar pit and eating cancer.

"What *is* that?"

"I used to think it was just about a relationship, but it's really all this shit; the way we keep fucking up the world. Earthquake, atom bomb, cancer. 'I've got a new complaint?' Get in line. I mean, one day it's just going to be flat earth outside."

"I always think that—whenever anything goes wrong." Did she? It sounded almost as though she was competing over who was more despairing, but she couldn't let him keep talking that way; it was too creepy. "Why aren't there helicopters?" she asked him. "If the police had it together, they'd be flying over to survey the damage and keep the looters under control."

"I've been hearing helicopters—haven't you?" Had she been asleep without realizing it?

"Maybe. But where are the searchlights?"

She told him about seeing Diane Keaton at the First AME Church the morning after the riots. The actress had been unloading shopping bags labeled "Matsuda" from her shiny new land yacht and Annabeth, in the back of a flatbed truck full of well-meaning West Siders, had found that funny. Later, after she'd spent the day shoveling ashes and collecting sodden drywall—and being looked at only with contempt by passing pedestrians—she decided the actress's form of contribution was no more self-deluding than her own.

David had been at a friend's place in Santa Barbara the night of the civil disturbance (as he called it), smoking pot with some high school friends. It was the last time he had ever, or would ever, smoke pot. "I had this image of my parents running into the fray, to offer free medical care and legal advice—because, you know, they're exactly the sort of people who would do that—and then before I knew it, I was picturing them being torn limb from limb by a pack of enraged black kids." Thinking of his mother, he knew how much she would be worrying about him right now. He wanted her to imagine him dead. He thought this, but he went on telling Annabeth the story he had begun: "We were sitting on the couch watching TV, and you could kind of see the mob behavior—except it was all shadowy, and who really knew what was going on? Then I looked over at my friend Philip, who *is* black. I realized I couldn't tell him any of what I'd been thinking, and *then* I remembered how weird my mother used to be around him when he came over in high school and I tried to apologize for that and he pretended not to know what I was talking about."

Annabeth nodded. She'd had no black friends in high school. She'd had no Jewish friends in high school. If David ever found out what a cultureless wasteland she'd grown up in, he'd probably reject her, completely. She hid her face in his armpit and he held her close, stroking her hair. They had been lovers for less than a year—there were a lot of stories they hadn't yet told each other. At dawn, they made love in a listless but soothing way and fell back to sleep afterward. When they woke up again, at eleven, they were sweaty and tangled in each other's arms and legs like drowned people.

The next morning, the front page of the *Los Angeles Times* reported twenty-five deaths and used "pancaked" to describe what had happened to an apartment building near the epicenter. Elsewhere, a construction worker had been rescued from underneath six feet of asphalt and a boy had been crushed by a building while his mother, in the next room, escaped unharmed. The Original Pantry restaurant, downtown, had continued serving all night, even in the dark. The mayor had imposed a curfew to discourage looting and had canceled the Martin Luther King Day parade.

Annabeth phoned Laura the following afternoon. She found her heart racing as she dialed. Did she really think Laura was dead? Her house was nowhere near Northridge, and it was unlikely that she'd been driving under some freeway overpass at four-thirty A.M. Yet she heard her own voice crack as she said, "It's me, Annabeth" to Laura's disinterested "Hello?"

Laura was, indeed, physically fine, as was Greg, but a eucalyptus bough had fallen on her car and their house had developed an alarming crack near the fireplace. She was waiting for a structural engineer to come assess the damage. Annabeth listened to the worst-case scenario that Laura had envisioned. Their house would be condemned but its true value was so much greater than what the insurance would pay that they'd be unable to afford a comparable new place to live—effectively homeless. They'd be strangled by legal bills and living in temporary housing and meanwhile she had a movie to produce. Annabeth felt out of her depth in the face of all this impending disaster, but she did her best to offer comfort. "Maybe it's really just a crack," she said.

"Not after the rains come in the spring," said Laura.

Part 3

ACTION

13

The acceleration of the *Trouble Doll* shoot—"from standstill to juggernaut in three days," Laura planned to say to interviewers—was the result of Steve Buscemi's unexpected decision to play the part of Jude, the sleazy actor. Buscemi had read the script and agreed to the job in a matter of hours, a highly unusual circumstance and a long-awaited gift, because, with Mr. Pink's funny blue-lipped face attached, the project became interesting to foreign investors. On the downside, Buscemi's availability for shooting was extremely limited, and if he was going to be part of the project it had to go "like, now," as Simpson put it to Laura. Unwilling to wait out additional offers, Simpson made a deal with Halo Pictures, an upstart company led by a former director of slasher films, two Israeli bankers, and three "power fetuses" with

MBAs. Halo had prenegotiated low-budget contracts with the unions, which saved *Trouble Doll* a good three weeks of prep time—plus, they were willing to let Simpson keep his sole "producer" credit. Laura cast an unknown young actress named Flynn Allison to play the part of Bunny, counting on her training at Yale more than her audition, and also on the soft transparency of her skin, which seemed likely to glow on film.

To Annabeth, it seemed that one night the sky had fallen and then, almost as soon as the rubble was cleared, her dream of working with Laura had suddenly come true. She'd been sitting on the back steps, stuck, intending to drive over to the Trader Joe's on National Boulevard but dreading its tiny congested parking lot and the problem of picking out wines that wouldn't make her look too cheap in David's eyes. The sunshine had already begun to slant obliquely, and she knew her failure to perform the one task she'd set herself for the day was starting to look pathological. And then the phone rang and it was Laura, breathless and ecstatic.

"We're going!" she said. It took Annabeth only a few heartbeats to understand who "we" were and the nature of "our" destination. She asked the next logical question: "When?" The whole phone call lasted no more than three minutes. There had been no doubt that Annabeth was available, or that the not-so-generous terms of the deal would be acceptable to her. In the course of the brief conversation, Annabeth heard herself reflecting Laura's exhilarated tone breath for breath, but when she got off the phone she felt a strange dissonance. There is a difference between asking someone to dance and telling them to do so, and Laura had done the latter.

———

Within days, Annabeth had hired an assistant, a guy who'd done the job on only two other features but came highly recommended. His name was Peter Calderon and he looked like a Mexican skateboard punk: shadow plaid shirt, long sideburns, Vans sneakers. She liked him on sight. Peter had the patience of a saint, everyone said. She left it to him to set up the machines, both digital (Avid) and manual (Moviola upright) and to order and install the rewinds, synchronizers, splicers, bins, and endless pairs of white cotton gloves that made a cutting room functional.

There was not a whole lot for Annabeth herself to do until footage started coming in, so she spent an inordinate amount of time making matching script notebooks for herself and Laura— three-ring binders that contained copies of the script as well as of the storyboards Laura had sketched for the few sequences that would require special equipment. The scripts were marked up with Annabeth's own notes regarding complete entrances and exits, careful matches for insert shots, and anticipatory solutions to other editorial bugaboos. She'd gone to three different stationery stores to find the kind of old-fashioned, blue canvas binders that could be written on directly with marker so that she could print the words "Trouble Doll" on the spines in her ultra-legible editor's handwriting. The finished product seemed impressive to Annabeth, a helpful tool in a handsome package. Simpson walked into the cutting room for the first time as she was admiring her work.

"Arts and crafts?" said the skinny strawberry-blond man in the too small suit.

"Uh, I guess so," said Annabeth, belatedly realizing, from his close physical resemblance to Tintin, that this man was, in fact, the producer. They had made her deal on the phone. "Hi, I'm Annabeth," she said, standing up to shake hands with him. He took her hand and led her to sit beside him on the nubby beige couch.

"Arthur Simpson," he said. "Nice to meet you finally."

"You, too," said Annabeth, studying his face, which seemed familiar, almost a version of her brother Jeff's.

"All set in here? Have everything you need?"

"I think so," said Annabeth. "They're delivering the Avid tomorrow—it's going to go over there."

"Great," said Simpson. "I hope you don't mind if I come in here to use the phone from time to time. It's really the only room with a door that shuts, isn't it?"

"Be my guest," said Annabeth, not at all comfortable with the thought of trying to cut the movie while the executive producer sat on the couch behind her making deals . . . but what could she say?

Simpson stood up again, "Well, just making the rounds. Only forty-eight hours left! I'm pretty excited, how about you?"

The way he looked at her then made Annabeth feel as though she had to make up for some past behavior—although she'd been nothing but effervescent in every phone conversation they'd had about her deal, and had done nothing at all wrong in the preceding minute or so.

"Oh, totally!" she said. "I haven't slept since Laura called me."

Simpson waved and stepped out of the cutting room. Annabeth sat down on the couch and tried to imagine the guy she'd just met pointing a gun at a woman. It seemed terribly unlikely.

———

The first morning of principal photography was an exterior at Trip and Bunny's run-down bungalow in Burbank. The only problem with the location was that it was across the street from a park that began to fill up with toddlers and their caretakers by midafternoon, so they had to get the exterior shots in before the real shrieking started. Annabeth arrived at six and placed Laura's notebook front and center on the table in the production trailer, along with a bunch of tulips in a mayonnaise jar and a picture postcard of a desert highway. As she sat there waiting for Laura to arrive, the craft-service kid came in and set up coffee and doughnuts on the same table, which kind of spoiled Annabeth's presentation, but it didn't seem right to interfere. When Laura came in—late, at six-twenty—Annabeth stood up and hovered while Laura, barely out of the trailer's stepwell, dispensed herself a cup of coffee.

"Hey," she said to Annabeth and then yelled out the trailer door to the first AD, "Is first team here yet?"

Annabeth couldn't hear the answer but picked up the notebook. "Here," she said, afraid that Laura would leave before she got a chance to present her gift.

"What?" Laura asked, turning abruptly to look at Annabeth.

"I made you this."

Laura looked at the notebook without apparent comprehension, but stepped forward into the trailer.

"It's a script."

"I have a script," said Laura, patting her shoulder bag.

"No, I know." Annabeth nodded. "I just marked this one up with some cutting notes."

Tim, the AD, stuck his head inside the trailer door. "Ten minutes," he said to Laura. "We're going to get the car pulling up and then turn around for Bunny slamming the door."

Laura nodded. "Great," she said, "I just want to walk it with Deke first." She threw her jacket onto the bench beside Annabeth, then reshouldered her bag in preparation for her talk with the cinematographer.

"Sorry, I guess I should have waited to do this," said Annabeth, realizing that she had lost her audience.

"To do what?" said Laura, patting herself down for her glasses.

"Nothing," said Annabeth. Laura nodded and stepped out of the trailer, opening the door wide, as though making an entrance for the benefit of anyone who happened to be outside watching. No one was until a grip with a massive white silk flag under his arm stepped out onto the liftgate of a truck parked across the street.

"Hey, cutie-pie," called Laura. Annabeth had never heard Laura speak that way to anyone, though she sounded perfectly natural. Then the trailer door shut and Annabeth was alone with Laura's script and a large vat of coffee. She decided to put the binder somewhere out of harm's way and, after some hesitation, wedged it spine outward between the cushions in the couch/daybed toward the rear of the trailer. She left the flowers where they were.

The next time Annabeth was in the production trailer, five days later, the script was exactly where she'd left it. Pink pages and blue pages had since been issued by the production office, but the copy she'd bound and marked up for Laura was still entirely white—untouched.

14

Earthquake damage on the 10 freeway forced Annabeth to explore new ways of driving across town. Neighborhoods she hadn't seen since she'd been a frequently lost L.A. newcomer came back into focus. An earlier, more authentic version of the city seemed to live on in the dingy pastel stucco, the borders of dusty Kaffir lilies and glossy, poisonous oleander. The mint-green Seaway Motel always caught her eye. It was so far from the ocean that Annabeth wondered whether its name referred to some inland body of water, now lost, like the Salton Sea. She could imagine how the Aloha Grocery, with its hand-lettered signs about homemade tofu, would have looked standing alone on its block, a destination instead of an oversight. The haggard House of Teriyaki Donut, the ingenious swimming-pool-blue painting of the airplane that was also a marlin at Centinela Travel, even the malevolent-sounding Shining Path preschool, set back in its shady yard: these sights made her nostalgic for a time and place that was wholly imaginary. Making her way east on Exposition Boulevard, she felt she should have been able to find an intersection with Flashback Drive, or Montage Way, but had to settle for Bundy, which took her exactly where she needed to go.

The *Trouble Doll* production offices and cutting rooms were at Big Time, a postproduction facility where Annabeth had worked many times before. It didn't look like anything from the street—if not for the sign, it would have been invisible. The large, single-story building, originally some kind of factory, contained three anonymous corridors lined with offices and editing suites. There were also a few independent producers' offices, an editing-equipment repair shop, and a screening room. Across the parking lot was a strangely ambitious split-level restaurant called Eureka, where the diners were dwarfed by an immense copper vat of microbrewed beer.

All Annabeth had to do at first was immerse herself in the raw footage as it came in. She watched the previous day's work first on the Moviola, her face pressed up against the tiny screen, her foot on the pedal that advanced the film. Getting her hands on the actual film every day was a ritual that kept her in touch with the privilege of her position. Thirty-five-millimeter film, even work print, even when backlit only by the Moviola's dim viewer, was an oil painting in comparison to the video she looked at while cutting on the Avid. Other than getting the dailies ready, her job during principal photography was to assemble the scenes as they came in, using the takes Laura had liked best on the set, and to put them in roughly the sequence in which they appeared in the script. This was the normal order of events on any feature film. By making this first assembly, the editor got acquainted with the strengths and weaknesses of the actors, the cameraman, the sound engineers, and so on. Then, when the shoot was over and the director came back to begin his or her first cut, the editor was expected to act as a well-informed set of hands. Only after the director's cut was complete would she get to dig in herself. But as Annabeth sat in her cutting room during the early days of *Trouble Doll,* she found herself straying from the plan. She would set out to assemble a sequence but find herself stopping to finesse some nuance, fine-cutting into dialogue and gesture before there was a scaffold of story on which to build. It was almost as though she wanted to get there first, but not to "win," just to prove Laura had done right by hiring her, that she was not only competent but talented.

During the second week of shooting, Laura dropped by the cutting room for an impromptu visit during an especially long lighting setup at a nearby location. Annabeth had just spent four hours working obsessively on a prickly insert shot that was supposed to reveal that one of Bunny's tips was a fifty-dollar bill. The master shot of Bunny into which the insert was supposed to fit never stopped moving, but the insert—of the rolled-up bill in an actor's hand—was static, and this destroyed the illusion of continuity. This was particularly irritating because it was one of the things she had made a note about in the script she'd marked up for Laura, and Laura had obviously never looked at that note. In any case, after trying to cut the insert numerous times, in numerous ways, that morning, Annabeth had engineered a solution that dispensed with the shot entirely. She had patched in a piece of added dialogue—"I gave her a fifty, let's see what I get"—which worked because you couldn't see the actor's face; the camera was over his shoulder, on Bunny. When Annabeth heard the cutting room door open and saw Laura, she felt a stab of excitement and anticipation: her friend would "get" the cleverness of this solution and praise her for it.

"Here, see what you think," she said, cueing up the footage as she stepped away from her chair at the Avid. Laura sat down and triggered the machine. Annabeth's work of art lasted about fifteen seconds. When it was over, Laura played it again. Then she shrugged.

"Can't you show me some of the assembly?" she said.

"Oh." Annabeth suddenly felt as guilty as she had previously been exalted. "I'm sorry," she said. "Let me set something up." And she began searching her hard drive for the pathetic beginnings of the assembly, reaching across Laura to tap the keys.

Laura got out of the chair, surrendering it to Annabeth. "That was a very weird little piece of film," she said to Annabeth's back. "Why did you show it to me?"

"I—I was just, I guess I was kind of proud of myself for writing a line of dialogue," said Annabeth.

"Yeah, leave that to the experts next time, huh?" It was a glib enough remark, not delivered with any particular venom, but it took Annabeth's breath away.

"I'm sorry," she said, her shame half-drowning her voice.

"It's no big thing," said Laura. "Look, if you've got performance anxiety, I sympathize, but it's time to get over it. Take a beta-blocker. I'd just like to see an assembly, okay?"

Annabeth nodded gratefully. Laura was right to be irritated. "I'll finish the first sequence today," said Annabeth. "You can see the all the club stuff and all the Trip's apartment stuff tomorrow after dailies, I promise."

"Perfect," Laura said, with only the faintest tinge of sarcasm.

At dailies that night, Annabeth found that the seating arrangement in the screening room had changed. On arriving, she had gone to the booth to remind the projectionist that the second reel contained a short end and to wait for it, and when she returned to her accustomed row, she saw that Simpson was occupying her usual seat while on Laura's *other* side, Simpson's daffy assistant, Lorelei, sat with notepad at the ready. There was no place for Annabeth at all. She thought she'd overheard Simpson mentioning Mia Goldman's name on the phone earlier in the week, but she'd dismissed it as paranoia. But that had been before Laura's visit to the cutting room. She was getting fired. The thing was to apologize. But how? Standing in the aisle at dailies she could hardly yell "I'm sorry" to Laura in front of everyone. Laura beckoned to Annabeth. This was it. But surely Laura was classier than to do it here, now?

"What are you doing?"

"Uh, I don't know where to sit."

Laura looked around and realized what had happened. "Move over," she said to Lorelei, with no more delicacy that she might have said, "You dropped this," and then nodded sideways at Annabeth, meaning *Sit down,* and said, "Let's get going."

The next night, as promised, Annabeth showed Laura what she had of the first assembly. Because the first location was Bunny's boyfriend's place, and then they'd redressed the same interior as Jude's apartment, the first complete sequence was the story's climax or culmination: the point at which Bunny realizes that she has burned all her bridges. Inside Trip's apartment, she learns that he has spent all the money she had saved to pay back her boss. Then she goes to see Jude, the actor who has been telling her he'll get her a meeting with a casting agent, and he essentially rapes her. After promising him that she will come back, that she is just going to score some meth, she goes back to Trip's, where she sees Sasha getting out of his car. He appears to be carrying a gun.

The sequence offered considerable drama—there was weeping, screaming, and attempted vehicular homicide. What bothered Annabeth about it, though, was Bunny. The actress was fine, but her story was a tale of such relentlessly wrong choices that every time her lips stopped moving, Annabeth found herself wondering whether anyone could be *that* stupid. This frustration was what gave the story "edge," according to Laura. (Annabeth had never understood what movie people meant by "edge." Speed? Anger? Irony?) Laura had also once said it was a film about longing, but longing required stillness and repose. Annabeth needed Bunny to stop moving and close her eyes, but she never seemed to.

Yet when Laura saw the assembled footage that night, she had no problem with Bunny or anything else. "That was fantastic!" she said.

Driving home after reviewing the sequence with Laura, Annabeth felt the accumulated tensions of the preceding two weeks overtake her. It was after midnight. As she crossed Ocean Park Boulevard, she gazed out toward the ocean but it was only an absence, a place where the city's lights stopped.

She knew David wasn't working that night, but for some reason she wasn't ready to see him, so she sat in her parked car listening to the radio call-in show *LoveLine*. The intimacy of hearing people's real voices and true stories in the middle of the night was soothing, for some reason. At least it was until one of the callers sounded like someone she knew, though she couldn't quite place who or where from. He called himself Paul, and he was talking about his compulsive need to have sex with a different stranger every day, in spite of being married to a woman he described as "brilliant, sexy, and up for anything, if you will." Annabeth didn't know any Pauls, but her sense that the voice belonged to someone she knew persisted, which made her uneasy about listening.

Dr. Drew, the show's "sensitive" interviewer, the one who always gave sound medical advice and made sure the real desperadoes got patched into the suicide hotline, told Paul that he was hurting himself and his wife with his behavior and that he should seek professional help. Paul thanked Dr. Drew politely and said he'd been in therapy since he was twelve. Dr. Drew's smart-ass sidekick laughed at that. "Nice one, Paul!" he said. "What's your complaint anyway? Sounds to me like you're getting more ass than Wilt Chamberlain." Annabeth hated the sidekick, but it was his crassness that finally enabled her to turn off the radio. In the silence that followed, her car's engine ticked, and she tried to close her eyes but she couldn't keep them shut. The night was too full of noises, and the pictures in her head were all bad.

15

In matching canvas chairs, Laura and Simpson waited in the courtyard of the 1920s apartment complex where they were supposed to be shooting a party scene. The illusion of dappled, rosy light emanating from strings of Chinese paper lanterns was taking an eternity to perfect. Amid dozens of extras, and a crew whose numbers were swelled by supplemental grips, electricians, and set decorators, both director and producer were doing their best to ignore the gathering sensation that their ship had run aground.

"This next bit's just a single and an over, right?" said Simpson, looking at his watch.

"Well . . ." said Laura, not yet ready to give up the empathetic effect she had hoped to achieve by following Bunny into the scene with a hand-held camera. Simpson was aware of this plan and was not at the point of asking directly for its sacrifice, but he wanted Laura to know it was on the table if they didn't start shooting soon.

"Hey, how was the assembly last night?"

"Fine. Except my editor's a passive-aggressive little cunt."

"Annabeth?" Simpson's voice cracked with an incipient laugh. Laura's head turned rapidly to check this.

"I'm serious. She decided she had to 'fix' the bit in the club from last week—before I'd even seen it cut together."

"Oh, stop. She worships the ground you walk on."

"As long she can walk in my footsteps—"

"Relax," he said, as he watched the cinematographer give a promising nod to the first AD. "Do you want me to talk to her?"

Laura shook her head and followed the slight shift in Simpson's focus toward the camera. The stand-ins were walking away, so she stood up. "But have you ever heard of that before? She even wrote new dialogue!"

"You never hear about anything an editor does that works, Laura. You know that."

She nodded at Simpson, but she was already forgetting about Annabeth as she walked back to the set, into the light, visualizing for the fiftieth time the material she was about to shoot. This was the scene that would take the curse off Bunny, that would make her an actor in her own life instead of a victim of circumstance. The traveling shot of Bunny making her way into the party—the lights and shadows on her face, the sense of motion and direction—would show the audience who she really was, how cunning and subtle. "Looks great," she told Deke, smiling. And when Flynn came out of makeup, the actress was so beautiful Laura wanted to kiss her.

Annabeth was careful to assemble the scene in the Chinese-lantern-bedecked courtyard according to Laura's notes. It was a lot of material and very little dialogue, but she could tell that Laura had a very specific idea about how the scene worked, and she did her best to reproduce it. It started with a shot of Bunny wandering into the crush of hipsters, reading the crowd and adjusting her appearance as she goes. Soon she decides that her bejeweled heels are too dressy, and she takes them off, proceeding barefoot toward the bar. Waiting for a drink, she begins to surreptitiously rub off her sparkly eye shadow, which is what she's doing when she spots Jude (Buscemi, doing a kind of Al-Pacino-in-*Scarface* number in white pants and a Hawaiian shirt). Subtly adjusting her décolletage before lifting her drink and crossing to him, she gets jostled by a dreadlocked guy but ignores him. She then sidles up to Buscemi and taps him, which is when the audience finally gets what it wants: a close-up of Bunny looking bewildered, smeared, and absolutely radiant.

But the volley of dialogue that came next—which had been filmed very late in the evening after long hours lighting and shooting the traveling shots—wasn't nearly as well executed. It seemed to veer from superficial flirtation into utter melodrama no matter how Annabeth put it together. The problem was not either actor's performance or even the move away from the subjective camera style at the top of the scene; it was the dialogue itself, which seemed to undercut Bunny's intelligence. She'd gotten herself this far—invited to the party—and she'd made contact with the guy who'd invited her. She should have stood pat and waited for his next move. Instead she turned into a dope, lowering her eyelids, confessing her dreams. "All I want is a chance" was the line that made Annabeth cringe. It wasn't even specific enough to be a real wish, just an open invitation to abuse—it was almost as though she was going to burst into song. The audience should feel that Bunny's sad end is inevitable, but not that she *deserves* it.

And so Annabeth had gotten bogged down in the details again, and that was when Laura, again, showed up unexpectedly. She opened the cutting room door without knocking, took one look at the Avid, and practically bounded up to Annabeth's side. "Oh boy, scene seventeen! Show me, show me!" she said, pulling up a nearby chair.

"It looks gorgeous," Annabeth said. She stopped herself from commenting on the dialogue, chastened after her experience with the insert shot in the strip club. Instead, she just ran the scene for Laura and stopped it after the fateful line.

"What's the problem?" said Laura.

"Well, it's like she's basically stripped off her clothes, hopped onto the sacrificial altar, and handed him the blade to cut out her heart with. It makes her a total victim," said Annabeth.

Laura nodded, as if to say "So?" Then raised her eyebrows and said, "Let's see the end."

Annabeth ran the tail of the scene for Laura, who snickered appreciatively at Buscemi's improvised alternative to "That's right": "Hey, I'm hip," he'd said.

"So, you think it's too soon in the story for her to be so . . . available?"

"Uh-huh," said Annabeth cautiously.

"Well, what if you bring up that bit with the Rastafarian spilling his drink? You know, step on her line with that business. Make it less of a walk-walk-walk, talk-talk-talk."

It was an excellent suggestion and a total mystery to Annabeth why she hadn't thought of it herself. She made a few quick edits and they watched the result.

"Yeah, like that!" said Laura. "I still have some cutting room chops."

"Thank God one of us does," said Annabeth.

Laura gave her an *Oh, please* look and said, affectlessly, "Teamwork, *n'est-çe pas?*"

Annabeth nodded.

"I'm going to get fired, I know it," she told David when he came in, at about four the next morning.

"Really?" he said, which was the wrong answer. He was supposed to reassure her. He could see on her face, even in the dark, that he had already fucked up. "Look, I don't know enough about the movie business to second-guess you. Whatever you tell me, I believe. So tell me what happened."

"I just keep getting myself into these things with Laura where she thinks I'm not on her side."

"How could she think that?"

Annabeth was silent, replaying the afternoon's conversation in her head. Why couldn't he just take her word for it and comfort her? Why did she have to explain? "Never mind," she said finally.

"It's only her second movie, right? I bet she's worried about what *she's* doing wrong. She probably thinks you're catching all her little mistakes and feels defensive." This was an excellent point, he thought, but Annabeth wasn't having it.

"She was working in cutting rooms while I was still an English major, David! I told you. Jerry Greenberg?"

She had told him. But what could he say now? "Do you even actually like her?"

"What?"

"You say she's your friend, but you never say anything nice about her. I mean, maybe you aren't on her side, really." It gave him a strange satisfaction to say this, although he knew it would enrage her.

Annabeth was speechless. After a few moments of stunned silence, she turned away, curling up into a ball. He felt his heart shrink.

Rolling onto his back, he felt a stab of pain in his injured foot—the wound was still open, and becoming infected. Tomorrow morning he would scrape away the dead tissue, flush it with hydrogen peroxide, and paint it with Betadine. "You'll get blood poisoning," his mother used to tell him when he picked his scabs as a boy. She sounded so certain, he had almost looked forward to the experience.

16

After the riots, jeeplike vehicles had started to proliferate on the streets of L.A., but after the earthquake—with the freeway out of commission for the foreseeable future and many canyon roads cratered and treacherous—the trend escalated geometrically. Every other car was a tank. Laura was not someone who usually entertained apocalyptic visions, but she sometimes found herself coveting an übervehicle too. That wish crystallized early one morning at the intersection of Beverly and La Cienega while she was waiting for the light to change. She realized she was being gazed down upon by the driver of a Range Rover and, moreover, that the onlooker was Jon Golden, her liar. Despite her light-hearted tone when discussing him with Annabeth, they had not parted on good terms—largely because Laura had made the mistake of sleeping with him, of falling in love with him, in fact. Now he seemed to be looking skeptically at her car, which was when she realized she was driving Greg's rusted Pontiac Firebird (the Karmann Ghia was in the shop, waiting for a part). Jon Golden was judging her on the basis of her husband's stinking heap of a car!

She couldn't roll down the window and yell, "It's not mine"—let alone "I'm directing a movie!"—because any attempt to explain would imply that the car really was hers, that she had something to compensate for. All she could do was pretend to ignore him, which she did, with all her might. As the light changed, Golden smiled and flickered his fingers, approximating a wave. The crew of *Trouble Doll* was turning around from days to nights—and her call time wasn't until four that afternoon. She was on her way to the cutting room to spend some quality time with her movie.

When Annabeth arrived at eight, she heard the muffled sounds of someone running her footage. She assumed it was Peter and gave him some time. She had often come in early or stayed late to study Janusz's work when she was assisting. Still, after dawdling over her coffee and looking at a few recent issues of *Variety*, she ran out of patience and tapped on the door. "Peter?" she said.

"Go away!" yelled Laura.

Annabeth immediately understood what had happened—faced with all those empty hours before call time, Laura couldn't stay away. That didn't make her curt dismissal any less wounding. But if the person in the next room had been any of the previous directors Annabeth had worked for—even the Idiot—she probably would have thought his gruffness justified. At any rate she would have found herself something useful to do while waiting to be called back in.

When Peter arrived at eight-fifteen, Annabeth asked him what he thought. How long did she have to wait before she could knock on the door again? "Forever," he told her. But he also pointed out that it sounded as though Laura was just running the assembly over and over. It was likely that no harm was being done.

"But I'm losing time!" said Annabeth. "I was going to cut the fucking fight scene this weekend. If I have to do that while we're doing dailies and everything, I'll never get through it."

"You don't have to prescreen the dailies, you know," said Peter. "I mean, I could just let you know if there was anything you really needed to look at beforehand."

Although this was true, it was not an acceptable answer. She wanted Peter to be on her side. She wanted to get into the Avid room *now*.

At three that afternoon, Laura finally emerged and called for Annabeth. "Hey," she said casually, as though the door had been open all along.

"Welcome back to daylight," said Annabeth, trying not to sound resentful. Then she noticed that the neck of Laura's T-shirt was stretched out almost to her shoulder. She had been compulsively picking at the skin on her back, where no one could see it if she bled. For a moment, Annabeth felt sympathy.

"You know how, sometimes, you just can't see what you're

doing anymore?" Laura asked. Annabeth nodded. "Would you come take a look?"

As she explained it to Annabeth, the top of the scene she'd been working on was fine, but she'd been thwarted by a bit of bad audio—an airplane had flown over and begun to drown out the line "C'mon, tell me where you hid the gun." Unfortunately, it sounded like "where you hid *them*" in the only other good-looking take, and in the only other usable piece of audio the actor had altered the line for emphasis, saying, "Tell me where you hid the fucking gun." Laura had tried to edit out "fucking," but she couldn't get it to match.

Annabeth believed that the problem Laura was *really* having was that she had reached a point in the script where the story foundered. Bunny wouldn't have hidden Sasha's gun. Bunny wouldn't have *touched* Sasha's gun. But there was no point in arguing that.

Laura waited anxiously for Annabeth to finish reviewing the scene. But when the editor was done she didn't bother to say, "The first part is great" or "I love how you finessed the business with the light," as she might have done with Peter. She just went with what she thought.

"Why don't you just play it on her?" she asked, meaning stay with Bunny during Sasha's line. Annabeth figured Laura had already tried this solution and found it wanting—it was Film Editing 101—but it was the only suggestion she had.

"Don't have it," said Laura.

Annabeth knew that they did. She wanted to throw the synchronizer at Laura's head—for lying, for wasting her time, for refusing to see what was right in front of her, which was that Anna-beth was the editor and she was out of line.

Laura giggled and shrugged in the ridiculous way Annabeth had sometimes seen her do with Simpson. It seemed to mean, *I abdicate all responsibility—you deal with it*. And then she got up from Annabeth's chair and left the room. And that was that.

17

Over the Presidents' Day weekend, Laura had to rewrite the scene of Bunny's audition, which was shooting the following week. To accomplish this, she decided she needed to be alone in the woods and had borrowed a friend's house near Lone Pine, where there would be snow on the ground and total silence in the air. To Annabeth's surprise, Laura invited her along on this trip. "You can get some air," she said. "You must be dying to get away from that *cell* at Big Time by now."

Annabeth wanted anything but that. There were only a few weeks left of shooting and therefore only a few weeks left during which she could work uninterrupted, but the invitation was too surprising, and too flattering, to turn down. When she saw the new Jeep Cherokee that Laura had just leased, however, she felt betrayed. She had pictured the two of them laughing and chattering in the tiny front seats of the Karmann Ghia, maybe even singing. But the new car seemed impersonal, outsized, and Laura had not even bothered to stock its state-of-the-art sound system with music. She had assumed that Annabeth would bring along cassettes of the songs they'd discussed for various sequences. So, almost the whole way there, they listened to KCRW, which Annabeth had all but stopped doing out of a perverse loyalty to David's show. She didn't want to know that Chris Douridas had recently made all the same amazing slush-pile discoveries that David had.

The borrowed house was huge, a genuine ranch on almost five acres of sheltered meadowland lined with mesquite and cottonwood. It was fully equipped with kitchen appliances, music, videos, even board games and puzzles, and it smelled like wood smoke and clay or, at any rate, like piñon incense. Annabeth was dying to determine who the owners might be, to look in their scrapbooks and see what they kept in their closets and their basement, but by four o'clock that afternoon, when the smell of marijuana smoke began to drift out of Laura's bedroom, she had pretty much exhausted the mysteries of the place. The owners were movie people, wealthy enough to have been photographed with Bill Clinton but otherwise unremarkable. Still restless, she set out for a walk. When she got past the half-mile-long driveway and out onto the road, Mount Whitney was looming darkly and the sky overhead looked cloudy and dramatic. She took deep breaths and tried to enjoy being outside—she always had as a child. But she felt exposed and unsafe on the side of the road; the traffic was infrequent but there was not much in the way of a shoulder, and

MY LIAR   127

the cars that did pass seemed much too close. The mountains are beautiful, she told herself, focus on the mountains.

When she had walked a mile or so along what turned out to be Highway 395, she caught sight of a green sign:

MANZANAR   8

INDEPENDENCE   18

It seemed to her like some beatnik poem. The word *Manzanar* itself was so exotic, like one of the destinations in the Crosby-Hope "Road to" pictures. *Manzanita* was the Mexican name for chamomile, she thought. The diminutive *ita* meant little—a little daisy? So was *Manzanar* the parent word? She pictured a town under the shadow of a giant daisy and smiled.

When she got back to the house, Laura was lying on the couch watching a tape of *Cutter's Way.* Her writing session had not gone well.

"Oh my God," said Annabeth, "I didn't know this was on video." She sat down on the floor in front of Laura, leaning her back against the base of the couch.

"I think it's a bootleg," said Laura, adjusting the throw covering her feet. "This is my favorite scene."

In the movie Jeff Bridges, sleek and youthful, had just come "home" to the ramshackle house he shares with his friends Cutter (a disabled Vietnam vet, played by John Heard) and Maureen (Lisa Eichhorn). His character, Bone, finds Maureen alone in the living room, drinking vodka by the fifth and weeping. "You look beautiful," he tells her. "Considering," she replies. As the scene continues, it becomes clear that there is a history of mutual attraction between the two old friends, and also some bitterness. At one point, Maureen reaches out in Bone's direction and he makes as if to take her hand, thinking she's coming on to him. "No," she says, reaching more directly for what she wants, "the bottle." Both women sighed at the beautiful bitterness of her performance.

"I wish I could make something even half that real," said Laura, which was where Annabeth was supposed to rush to the fore with reassurance, but she missed her cue. "I *said*, I wish I could make something even half that real . . ." she repeated, now making fun of herself but still demanding her fealty.

"You have?" answered Annabeth, and then, "I mean, you are!" which made them both laugh.

"So, where'd you go, before?" asked Laura.

Annabeth described her walk and, feeling expansive, began to extemporize about the evocative mileage sign: Dorothy Lamour, the giant daisy . . . and just a little farther on, independence. "Isn't that kind of great?" she asked.

"Great?" Laura sounded irritated. "Manzanar was a fucking concentration camp for Japanese-Americans. Are you some kind of moron?"

"No, I mean, I knew that," Annabeth lied. "I just meant the words . . . the juxtaposition on the sign . . ." Annabeth felt slapped in the face, but also as though she'd asked for it. No one ever seemed to tell her anything she "should have" known: that children couldn't sign their parents' checks, that it was rude to stare, that girls didn't wear Y-front long johns, and on and on. She always had to find out for herself, and invariably someone found her mistake not just ignorant but offensive. It was probably why she'd made a career out of something no one in her high school graduating class was ever likely to know more about than she did.

Laura got up from the couch and turned off the VCR. As she did, Annabeth began nervously straightening the items on the coffee table: copies of *Vanity Fair* and *Daily Variety,* Laura's barely scribbled-on yellow pad, the video box . . .

"Do you have any idea how irritating it is when you do that?"

"Do what?" asked Annabeth.

"Oh, don't mind me, I'll just straighten up a few things," Laura said in a squeaky voice. "I'm just a little mouse with obsessive-compulsive disorder."

"I just—" Annabeth's voice sounded strangled. "I mean, we're going to have to make the place neat again before we leave . . . so why not do it as we go?"

"Because I'm here to relax, that's why. And when we leave is hardly the point. You do it in the cutting room, too—you do it in my fucking office, for crying out loud."

Annabeth could feel her cheeks blotching red, the way they always did right before she started to cry.

"Oh, no," said Laura.

"I can't help it," said Annabeth, her voice thick.

"Why do I always end up taking care of *you?*" Laura said, getting up to find some tissues for Annabeth, mostly as a way to avoid watching her face crumple any further. But Annabeth's reaction was arrested by Laura's remark. She had said the same words to David the week before.

The next morning, Laura took Annabeth to Lone Pine proper for a diner breakfast. As they sat at the table, waiting for their coffee,

Annabeth wondered if this was going to be the Dear John breakfast. After she'd come out of her bedroom that morning, Laura
hadn't said much of anything except "Do you want to go to town
and get something to eat?" The next thing she knew, they were in
this little café that might as well have been on the Iron Range, ordering eggs and pancakes and bacon. Annabeth finally forced herself to look up and attempt to smile, but as she did so, she saw
that Laura was staring out the window in a trance of abstraction.
Then Laura refocused, smiling amiably. "Let's go to Manzanar,"
she said.

"Really?" said Annabeth.

"Yeah, it's right there. I've never been. Let's go."

But Manzanar had been erased. There was an obelisk, and a
plaque, and a pervasive sense of desolation, but the scouring
wind had taken care of the rest, whatever the rest had been. They
couldn't even tell how big the site was. The wind felt as though it
were being piped in from some other climate, some arctic region
just out of sight. Annabeth was wearing a wholly inadequate
denim jacket, but she had a hat on, which helped. Laura, in
leather, was better protected, but her hair was getting whipped
into such a frenzy that she couldn't even read the plaque and,
anyway, she wasn't wearing her glasses. She asked Annabeth to
read the inscription aloud, which she did, yelling to be heard over
the gale.

" 'In the early part of World War II, a hundred and ten thousand persons of Japanese ancestry were interned in relocation
centers by Executive Order No. 9066, issued on February 19,

1942. Manzanar, the first of ten such concentration camps, was bounded by barbed wire and guard towers, confining ten thousand persons, the majority being American citizens.' " Annabeth stopped reading to consider the number: one hundred and ten thousand? She looked at Laura, trying to picture how many people that actually was, how many families. Laura just nodded, as if to say "Go on," so she continued.

" 'May the injustices and humiliation suffered here as a result of hysteria, racism, and economic exploitation never emerge again. California Registered Historical Landmark No. 850. Plaque placed by the State Department of Parks and Recreation in cooperation with the Manzanar Committee and the Japanese American Citizens League, April 14, 1975.' " Well, if the state of California hadn't put up a plaque until 1975, she wasn't *that* ignorant for never having heard of the place.

The two women took a silent walk around the site, seeing remnants of building foundations as well as some strangely incomplete examples of recent care—the one remaining building had black plastic sheeting in its window frames, and a small patch of garden seemed to have been recently fenced and weeded, though nothing grew. Ultimately, it was too cold to linger and too windy to talk and they got back in the Jeep, grateful for its blasting climate-control system and heated seats.

When Annabeth got home the next day, she found David lying on the couch watching television. She had the feeling it was all he'd done all weekend.

"What do you know about Manzanar?" she asked him.

David shrugged. "I've never been there, but there are some great photographs. Ansel Adams, or someone like that. People there making the best of it, dancing, playing softball . . ." He could rattle all this off without removing his eyes from *The X-Files*.

"For how long?"

"I don't know. Forty-one to forty-three or -four?"

"What do you mean, 'dancing'?"

She could see him struggling with his disinclination to abandon the exploits of Dana Scully. The show was on tape, though, so the conversation with the returning girlfriend obviously trumped it. He sat up and pressed the pause button on the remote.

"Didn't you learn about this in school?"

"No, I didn't," Annabeth said, collapsing into the canvas butterfly chair beside the couch.

"Well, you know, they moved whole families there, whole neighborhoods, so people did their best to build up some kind of normal life, I guess. There are pictures of, like, people gardening, and high school proms, and young men in uniform making brave good-byes . . . the whole thing."

"What kind of uniforms?"

"Military uniforms? You know, the war?" Now he sounded sarcastic, which made Annabeth want to throw something. But she didn't. The idea of having to re-create "normal" life from scratch in that desert of creosote and alkali was fascinating to her. She pictured herself as a young girl, playing alone in an imaginary shantytown at the Manzanar site. She pictured herself scrubbed clean and dressed in the 1940s version of a prom dress, on the arm of a skinny Japanese boy. She pictured herself weeping, saying good-bye to the boy, now in uniform. Then she emended—not weeping, waving stoically. Looking again at David, she remembered his mother's murdered parents. It was disgusting to invent tragedy, she told herself, but the Japanese boy still looked back at her with sad eyes.

18

One morning in March, Annabeth found Simpson sitting on the couch in her cutting room, returning phone calls. It was not the first time; he seemed to like having the background noise on his calls, frequently apologizing to his callers in very specific terms ("Sorry about the playback," "Forgive me, I'm calling from the cutting room here"). What was unusual was that when he saw her on this particular morning, he started gesturing furiously for her to wait, indicating that he had something important to tell her, or perhaps that the building was on fire—all she could really figure out was that he was excited and, for some reason, she was the one he wanted to tell about whatever was exciting him. She walked up to the Avid and switched it on, still watching him, nodding, smiling, not sure whether or not she was supposed to sit down and start working.

"No, no, that's unacceptable," Simpson was saying, grinning like a jack-o'-lantern. "I'll get it from somewhere else then." And then to Annabeth, with his right hand still holding down the telephone's hook switch: "It looks like I've got Oscar tickets. Wanna come?"

It was not a question anyone in their zip code, or in any of the five surrounding zip codes, would even blink before answering in the affirmative. Only after he'd left did Annabeth begin to ponder the ramifications of having accepted: Why hadn't he asked Laura first? How could she drive up to the Dorothy Chandler Pavilion in her battered Honda? What on earth would she *wear*?

She was saved the trouble of explaining the circumstances to Laura by Simpson himself. "I hope you don't mind—I'm taking your editor to the Oscars with me," he told her over lunch at Campanile, secretly gleeful as her cool gold eyes widened noticeably, which had been the whole point. He'd heard that Jon Golden had recently been shopping around a project with Laura attached, a project that they wanted to start as soon as *Trouble Doll* wrapped, reportedly. Taking Annabeth to the Oscars was his way of letting Laura know that her disloyalty had consequences.

The next morning, Simpson was back in Annabeth's room to commence preparations. "Hey, what's your dress size?" he said.

"My what?"

"I've got a friend at Calvin Klein—they'll comp you a dress if your size hasn't been all grabbed up by the stampede of ingenues."

"What do you mean, comp me a dress?"

"Loan it to you, for free, to wear to the Oscars. Everyone does it."

"What if I spill something?"

Simpson laughed. Annabeth didn't. "I won't let you near anything that stains, how's that?"

Gifts always made Annabeth uncomfortable, but was this a gift or just a professional courtesy? She was on a tight schedule, she was supposed to be working—didn't he get that?

He continued: "I think a dove gray or a very pale yellow. Or white? What do you think?"

"I have no idea?" Her rising inflection seemed to imply something else, but what she said next was "I generally stick with white, black, and locker room grey."

"Black would wash you out completely—we have the same coloring, in case you haven't noticed." And then he left, as suddenly as he had appeared. A few hours later, Laura appeared in the doorway, noisily swirling an iced coffee.

"I think yellow is a good idea," she said to Annabeth's back. Annabeth didn't know what she was talking about. Laura continued, "For the dress. It's television—you need a color to even be visible." She seated herself on the spare swivel chair and crab-walked it up beside Annabeth's.

Annabeth didn't want to discuss her Oscar date with Laura. It didn't feel safe at all. Which was too bad, because she didn't know anyone with better taste in clothes. "Really?" she tried, weakly.

"Oh, come on, live a little, Annabeth. You're going to the Oscars!"

"What would *you* wear?"

"Something fabulous."

Annabeth nodded, trying to translate "fabulous" into an item she could picture.

"What about pink," Laura went on. "You can wear pink, can't you?"

"Can we talk about something else?" said Annabeth. Laura laughed and swayed back and forth a bit, using her feet to pivot.

"Is he hiring a limo?" she asked.

"I don't know."

"What parties are you going to, after?"

"Oh, come on, Laura. I'm not going anywhere. I feel bad enough about leaving David home as it is."

"David's not in the industry—what does he care?"

"Wouldn't you bring Greg if you could?"

Laura considered. "No," she said, biting her lip as though it hurt her to admit it. "I'd bring someone I could order around, who would step back when the photographers queued up . . . someone like you." It was an evil remark, but Laura delivered it with a lightness that belied that.

"Are you mad at me?" asked Annabeth.

Laura snorted, then stood up. "What is this, fifth grade?"

This was one of those no-win conversations. She used to have them all the time with her mother. "Well, if you ever are, I hope you'll tell me," she said, but the line reading seemed unconvincing.

A few days later, Annabeth and David were looking at the Sunday paper. The Calendar section was full of Oscar-related stories.

"Maybe I should just beg off," said Annabeth. David didn't have to ask what she was talking about.

"Do you think he's going to make a pass at you or something?" he asked.

She didn't. The thing that made her uneasy about Simpson was less obvious than that, although sexual discomfort was also part of it. There was something about the way he treated her that was so . . . avuncular? As though he'd known her all her life, read her diary, seen her naked—none of those were it, but all of them were close. She even sometimes imagined that he was her half sibling, a member of the family her father must have decided he liked better in the end. She'd never told anyone about the other-family theory, though, and now seemed like the wrong time.

"So, I don't get it," David said. "Isn't this the senior prom? Haven't you always wanted to go?"

She had. Annabeth nodded and looked again at the newspaper page in front of her. The Best Actress nominees were pictured: Holly Hunter, Emma Thompson, Stockard Channing . . . Lion-faced Laura would've wiped the floor with any one of them, looks-wise. Annabeth had never seen Laura in a dress, let alone a gown, but she was sure the effect would be stupendous. David hadn't shown any interest at all in what Annabeth was going to wear—she hadn't perceived the first sign of jealousy on his part. *She* would have been insanely jealous if the shoe was on the other foot. David smiled at her as he reached for the Sports section. Everything looked jolly, over at his end of the table. Why was she so uptight?

"Do you think it's too late for me to ask Laura to go in my place?"

"Uh, isn't that Simpson's call? I mean, they're his tickets."

"I could tell him I thought it was a bad career move for me."

"Yeah, but wouldn't that kind of imply that dissing him was more acceptable than dissing Laura?" He had a good point.

When Annabeth had first arrived in L.A., she had been astounded by the beauty and abundance of the place: the flowers, the palm trees, the almost pornographic displays of produce at the market—it seemed to promise an endless parade of more and better. And to some extent it had delivered. Eight weeks ago she had been on the threshhold of everything, of the life she thought she'd always wanted, and now she was even going to the Oscars. But somehow the exaltation, the adrenaline and wonder, had burned off as mysteriously as the morning fog. Anyone could go to the Oscars, it turned out, even Annabeth—so then what? "You come looking for Hollywood," Janusz had once told her, "but you wind up in Los Angeles, and this is the problem."

19

The day he heard that Kurt Cobain was in a coma in Italy, David reopened the wound on his foot to clean it with a penknife. The skin had healed over but badly, and it still felt tender. It gave readily under the less-than-razor-sharp blade, but he couldn't find anything trapped there—no pus, no pebble, no excuse for limping around.

He had been asleep when the radio came on, so the news about Kurt (he thought of him as a friend) reached him in that state where dreams mix easily with information from the world outside. In David's half sleep the news about Kurt's coma resulted in a dream about a heart-shaped reliquary—a jeweled box containing bits of jagged bone and gouts of flesh. He knew that the item was precious and closed it up again, quickly hoping he had not harmed it—maybe the box itself was an organ, a life. In David's childhood home, too much attention to one's body was frowned upon, even when one was spanking clean and in robust health, perhaps especially then. He was not supposed to be naked, except in the bath. Kurt's songs felt like the antidote to that sense of physical shame. They brought the body's effusions and illnesses into the daylight. He didn't like the thought of their author in a Roman hospital.

And, though he had carefully sterilized the knife blade on the front burner of the old O'Keefe and Merritt stove, David's foot was soon infected.

Annabeth drove her beat-up Honda only as far as Simpson's case-study-style house in Mount Washington on Oscar night. As it turned out, Simpson's Calvin Klein connection was not as solid as he had hoped, so he had rented Annabeth a gown from a resale shop in Beverly Hills, correctly assuming that she would never know the difference. It was extraordinarily simple, a beautiful pale gray, and if it had been properly altered for her it would have swooped where it unfortunately sagged. Annabeth had no ass to speak of. Simpson had also hired Inga, the makeup "artist" from *Trouble Doll,* to do Annabeth's face while she sat on a barstool in his kitchen and he chatted inanely. It was the first time she had ever been professionally made up and the sensation was so intimate she almost couldn't bear it. When Inga was finished with Annabeth, she also dusted some sparkly stuff on Simpson, who giggled like a schoolgirl. It was then that Annabeth realized they were both high on coke.

Sitting in the Town Car a few minutes later, Annabeth knew

she should be feeling like Cinderella but she kept thinking of Maria in *Lost Horizon,* whose illusion of youthful beauty was destroyed as soon as she stepped across the invisible boundary between Shangri-La and the real world. The drive to the Music Center seemed endless. For almost an hour, they spasmed along—going five miles an hour, then twelve, then seven—even after they were within easy walking distance of their destination. No one would dream of walking up to the Oscars. Annabeth doubted that it was even possible. Instead, they sat in their little metal box surrounded by other cars—all spewing exhaust and radiating heat—and Annabeth could feel her makeup start to melt and her nervous sweat start to soak the armpits of the dress (which she still mistakenly believed was worth more than she earned in a month). She looked over at Simpson. Thank God it wasn't an actual limo, she thought; if she'd had to sit facing him the whole time she would have given up before they even got there, or would at least have broken into the cut-glass decanter of cheap vodka in the fold-down bar. Of course that was probably just a prop.

Simpson, meanwhile, was gazing out the window quite happily, tapping out a little rhythm on the knee of his disinterested-looking Jil Sander tux. He felt her gaze, but didn't turn. "Isn't this wicked cool?" he said.

"I'm a little bit intimidated," said Annabeth, and thought, *Duh.*

"That's the fun part." Then he turned toward her. "Couple of kids from the Great Plains at the big tent."

"You've never been to the Oscars before?"

"Are you kidding?"

"So how'd you get the tickets?"

"Friend from film school who works in Penny Marshall's office."

And then he did something completely bizarre. He tickled her. Just stuck an index finger into her midriff and voilà! Annabeth giggled. She couldn't remember the last time she had done so. Smirked, chuckled, snickered, sure, but the high-pitched trill that she heard come out of her throat in the Town Car was none of the above. She braced herself for further incursions—wasn't that how tickling went?—but Simpson looked entirely satisfied with himself. Maybe he really was her imaginary half brother.

They walked along the red carpet with everyone else—to Annabeth's surprise, there was no side entrance for the nonfamous; the TV cameras just somehow shot around them. Annabeth took note of the stupendously Irish-looking old guy from *In the Name of the Father,* who was surrounded by reporters—he was a nominee in the supporting category. Then they passed Christina Ricci from *Addams Family Values,* who was attempting to attract the attention of a camera crew with a come-hither smile out of all proportion to her tiny presence. Simpson appeared to *tsk* this sight as they went by. But traveling at a normal pace, they were off the carpet and into the building before Annabeth had even had a chance to realize that the normal-enough-looking guy on her right was Jeff Bridges, her idea of someone actually worth ogling.

Their seats were in the second balcony, a circumstance it had never occurred to Simpson to anticipate and that he found almost intolerable once they were seated. She could see him hunching down with his hand on his forehead, hiding his face from the people seated around them—as though it mattered to them where the white-rat-looking guy and the scrawny girl in the baggy dress were sitting. Their presumed onlookers were just the extended families of the sound, editing, documentary, and short-film nominees, after all. Here and there, Annabeth even saw faces she recognized (from life, not television or film)—six sound editors had been nominated for *The Fugitive* alone, and God only knew how many special-effects guys. But she could sense that Simpson did not want her waving or beckoning so she, too, laid low. Which left her not much to do. They were miles away from the stage, and even to follow along on the nearby TV monitors required a degree of neck craning that soon defeated her. As the evening went on, Annabeth found herself dozing. At the Oscars! Appalled, she undertook a foray to the ladies' room.

Down several flights, below orchestra level, she found a large lounge area and a small refreshment stand. A hodgepodge of people were there watching television monitors with the same bonhomie as home viewers—Annabeth could hear the familiar undercurrent of wisecracks, mystified observations, and strangely attenuated murmurs of affection. She would have had to stride across the vast room to join them, though, and that would have required a bolder personality than the one she was stuck with. Instead, she made a beeline for the ladies' room, where Sally Field was washing her hands and chatting loudly with an invisible someone who sounded an awful lot like Bette Midler. Annabeth quickly immured herself in the booth nearest the door and waited. Movie-star gossip! In person!

"Yeah, I don't know, it looked a lot better in the can," said the Midler soundalike.

"How do you mean?" asked Field.

"One sec, I have to figure out how to get this damn thing back around without dipping my train . . ."

"Just flush. I'll help you straighten your train out, darling," Field said.

"Well then!" said Midler, and flush she did, drowning out most of the interchange that followed. Still, Annabeth had heard enough to deduce that the can in question contained a paint color and not a feature motion picture. Unless someone was about to release a movie called *Tuscan Putty,* but that seemed unlikely. On her way back up the stairs she tried avidly to reconstruct the moment as something she could retell to Simpson, but it had almost nothing going for it as an anecdote, except maybe its lack of anecdotal content. It didn't matter, because when she had finally sweated her way back up the four flights of stairs, Simpson took one look at her and said, "Let's go. At least we'll beat the traffic."

On the way back down, they passed Oliver Stone loitering on a landing. He smiled and nodded, seeming to suggest that Annabeth and Simpson were rushing off to have hot sex with each other. Annabeth found herself turning to look back over her shoulder at the director, wanting to clarify—*No, it's not that at all.* But Stone just nodded again, and also winked.

And that was it. The night of glamour and giddiness was over. She stopped at Simpson's just long enough to remove the unharmed evening gown, wrap it in its tissue, and return it to its box. When she got back to Venice, David was engrossed in his usual activity: sampling the ever-more-giant pile of freebie CDs that were now his work—as though it were a night like any other. She got his attention when she came in, but he was the wrong audience for her debrief.

"So, did you see me?" she asked.

"You were on TV?"

He'd spent the early part of the evening at his sister Linda's in Larchmont. Her rambling mansion of a house would not have been remotely affordable until after the riots, and since the earthquake it had been half-swathed in black Duvateen (the roof leaked) and adrift in various types of dust. While she and her husband and their friends had watched the awards show in the den, David had sat on the living room floor, trying to sort through the *Encyclopaedia Britannica,* which he had always thought of as *his* until Linda had taken it to Larchmont, and which had thus been battered during the earthquake. Pages were torn and spines were broken. Smoothing out the wrinkled leaves and dusting off the covers was David's idea of the perfect antidote to the inane chatter of Oscar night, and as soon as he was done with that project, he left. He knew it was good for Annabeth's career that the producer liked her enough to take her to the Oscars, and also that it was good for Annabeth's career to *go* to the Oscars, and to whatever parties might follow, but he hadn't really wanted her to do any of it. He'd wanted her to sit with him on his sister's floor, examining encyclopedia volumes and making fun of the big kids on TV. On his way back to Venice, driving through the strangely deserted city, David had decided that the movie business and the music business had no legitimate relation to each other—they just happened to occupy the same county. Within the music business (which also had the propensity to become odious; he couldn't deny that) working as a DJ on public radio was, if he wanted to stretch the point, as clean and blameless as you could get. He was a music lover, not a unit shifter.

"I was standing right next to Christina Ricci on the red carpet," Annabeth said, still trying to interest him.

"Who's Christina Ricci?"

But she knew that he knew—he had loved the scene in which Wednesday told her summer camp bunkmates a ghost story so terrifying that it made them scream in true horror. His denial now made Annabeth laugh—it was such a perfect David moment. His Eeyore-sounding voice, his prickly lack of interest in Hollywood—these were the things about him that she loved. Sometimes she forgot.

And David was sorry to have missed seeing his girlfriend in her beautiful getup on TV; he just couldn't say so. There were still traces of makeup on her face—just some mascara and sparkly gray stuff at the corners of her eyes—but he could tell that she'd been exquisitely beautiful just a few hours before and he'd missed it. It made him want to kill and eat that Simpson guy.

Annabeth went into the bedroom and telephoned Laura, who *had* seen her editor's infinitesimally brief appearance on national television. Laura had recorded the red carpet and had reviewed the tape repeatedly for signs of Simpson's arthritic cowboy gait. She loved the part about the seats in the peanut gallery and Simpson hiding his face. She also loved the part about Oliver Stone's insinuating looks. "You should have told him you went to Yale," she told Annabeth.

"But I didn't," Annabeth said.

"Yeah, I know, but he's one of those assholes who think you have to have an Ivy degree to breathe the same air he does."

"We were just passing on the stairs."

"You probably could have gone home with him if you'd wanted to."

"I didn't want to."

"Oh, play along!"

"Okay."

"So what else?"

But there was nothing else. She'd only wanted sympathy for having somehow alienated her boyfriend and depressed her producer in the same night, through no fault of her own that she could discern. And she wanted someone, anyone, to celebrate with her—she'd been to the Oscars, she'd worn an evening gown, Oliver Stone had winked at her!

Annabeth lay awake in bed that night wondering what her mother would have thought. Not that she expected her mother to have watched the thing—Eva didn't care for television. She would have spent the evening reading some book about medieval Europe, obtained at great pains from interlibrary loan. But if Annabeth presented the evening the right way—not too self-impressed, a little bit woeful—she might be able to discern some trace of pride leaking out among her mother's clipped queries and skeptical "hmmphs." She didn't call and try this, though—it was too risky. Feeling how she felt was not perfect, but it was better than feeling destroyed.

Eva Jensen *was* proud of her daughter, if only—well, mostly—for getting out of the northern Midwest. No one else in her family

had ever gotten south of Green Bay. Eva herself was still living in
the same large, cold house Annabeth's father had left her in
twenty-three years earlier, and she still resented every minute she
spent sitting in that living room, being ticked at by the brass-and-
cherrywood clock that had belonged to Gus's mother. At first,
she'd thought he'd eventually have to return for it—and she'd
kept it wound and polished, in perfect condition, against that possibility. But as the years had passed, she came to realize that if
Gus did return, it would not be until Eva herself was good and
dead. Still, she kept winding the clock, and polishing it, and waiting.

20

Scene 11 was the hardest part of the movie for Annabeth. She worked on it for almost two solid days. It was a fight scene and she had never cut one before, and this made her insecure. But she did remember Janusz's recipe—"A fight is just a conversation with fists"—and that was enough to get her started.

The fight was supposed to gradually build to the moment when Trip punched Bunny in the face. The most difficult part was cutting it so the audience would believe the actor's timid shove was a real slam, because Bunny was going to have a black eye in scenes 12 and 13. Unfortunately, at the end of a long night of hard work in close quarters, Laura had let Deke talk her into shooting Trip's final punch only from angles beside and underneath Bunny's head.

When Annabeth had finally gotten the rest of the scene to

work, it seemed painfully obvious to her that Deke's "Dutch angles" made the moment seem more humorous than painful. And
the sequence came early enough in the picture that this unin-
tended humor could skew the whole tone of the movie.

When she finally cracked it, she felt like a genius. She started
with a staccato series of back-and-forth cuts that got faster as the
argument escalated. Then, just before Trip's shoulder moved, she
went into a close-up of his face for an extra-long beat. She stole
this close-up from a completely different scene in which the actor
playing Trip had flubbed his line, but she found she could use
the slack expression on his face to supply the vicious subtext for
the punch. She knew that, because of what had come before, the
viewers would project the buildup of rage that the scene needed,
even though what he was really thinking was something more like
Uh, what was that line again?

But something still wasn't right. The punch still lacked impact.
Frustrated, she lopped off the last shot entirely, so that the scene
ended just after Trip's shoulder flinched. She told herself she
would watch it again the next morning, when fresh eyes might
suggest what should come next, but then she ran it one more time
and saw something else. The absence of a final blow was, in itself,
a solution. It left an unanswered question hanging over the rest of
the movie, a subconscious desire to see that last punch land. And
that uneasy suspense would make Bunny's violent death feel like a
relief as well as an affront when it finally came. "Always, if possible, make two emotions at once," Janusz had taught her, and at last
she had done it. Laura seemed to get it when she showed it to her,
but all she said was "Nice work. I think we still need a meatier
sound effect for that first one, though."

21

Annabeth set up the first recruited screening of *Trouble Doll* for
four in the afternoon at the Art Theatre in Long Beach.

"We're doing it *where*?" Laura snarled in disbelief. The location indicated to her that Halo Pictures had decided to dump her
film. Why else test it with a demographic destined to find it, at
best, mystifying?

"It's a beautiful old Deco theater, you'll like it," said Annabeth.

"I don't fucking care how beautiful the theater is, it's Orange
County. They'll all be Republican retirees. What were you thinking?"

Laura had assumed that Annabeth was smart enough to run
interference with Halo's publicity harpies—lipsticky women in
suits who had suggested the Art because it was close to the South

Bay towns where they all happened to live. She believed that, as the film's editor, Annabeth should have raised objections about the quality of the projection, the audio system, any number of technical things the marketing bitches wouldn't know how to rebut. All Laura could do was whine, no matter how successfully she modulated her voice.

From Annabeth's point of view, the farther the screening was from her own neighborhood and demographic, the more easily she could distance herself from whatever hurtful things the viewers might write on their little blue cards. It was her assumption that The Director was the one who could push the studio around when it came to questions of marketing and promotion. If Laura was so unhappy about the Art, why didn't *she* throw some weight around?

So: Long Beach it was. And, as in every cutting room Annabeth had ever worked in, everything seemed fine until the night before, when the director finally started to understand that the film was about to face the eyes of strangers. Like the rest of them, Laura then began a fusillade of picture trims, dialogue lifts, and sound-effect tweaks that it fell to Annabeth both to execute and to keep track of in case Laura decided later to revert. The problem was exacerbated by Laura's conviction that, because she remembered how to operate the Avid, she was still a competent editor. At eight-fifteen that evening she took over Annabeth's chair and, when she could no longer bear the sense of her editor breathing down her neck, she asked, or perhaps told, Annabeth to go get her a sandwich.

"Sure," said Annabeth. "I'll send Peter."

"No," said Laura. "I don't trust him."

Annabeth thought Laura meant that she didn't trust Peter with petty cash, which he'd been spending frugally and keeping very good track of for more than three months at that point and which assertion offended Annabeth on principal. Hearing no answer, Laura turned momentarily away from the Avid and saw the appalled look on Annabeth's face.

"No, I mean I don't trust him to pick out a good sandwich. He's a guy."

"Well, just tell me what kind you want and he'll get it."

"Just a sandwich, you know, tuna fish or turkey or something."

It was already after eight and Annabeth was hard put to even think of a nearby deli that was open. In some ways, the easiest thing would just be for her to drive home and make the sandwich herself. And, after five minutes of cruising around West L.A., that was exactly what she did. By the time Annabeth got back, Laura was no longer interested in food, though. She'd decided to make a few more "tiny" changes and Peter was dutifully logging the conformations. They went home at midnight.

The day of the screening, Laura "slept in" unsuccessfully while Annabeth and Peter got the film ready to go—cleaning it, reinforcing the splices, adding leader, and labeling the reels. The screening itself was at four in the afternoon, and by two they were ready to roll. Until Annabeth put up reel 3 for one last look at the night-sky effect they'd gotten back from the optical house the preceding morning. Peter bit his tongue.

The 10 was still closed, so Laura decided to drive to Long Beach on surface streets—mainly Alameda Avenue. She'd never before taken this street much past downtown, where it was a wide road that moved quickly, but on the map it appeared to go directly to her destination via a sequence of thinly populated ex-suburbs. It had to be better than the 110, she figured. Greg warned her that, in effect, taking Alameda was taking the Blue Line and she should expect to stop as often and as miserably as she might if riding L.A.'s proud, empty prototype for a new era of rapid transit. She asked him when the last time he'd taken the Blue Line was, knowing the answer was "never."

As it turned out, what got in her way was not vehicles but rubble—truckloads of it. On a small side street in Huntington Park, a local entrepreneur had created an ad hoc waste-management site that had become the final resting place for the remains of the earthquake-ravaged Santa Monica Freeway. Truckloads of the stuff trailed plumes of pulverized asphalt in a steady parade. The dumping ground, already known locally as La Montana, was almost a hundred feet high. Laura, a childhood asthmatic, got herself trapped between two rubble-laden tractor-trailers on their slow, gritty way to the pile. It was a hot afternoon and the Karmann Ghia, which she was driving "for luck," was laboring under the effort of generating cool air. If she turned off the AC she'd have to open the window, but if she opened the window she feared her lungs would close up. She was sweating, her new Belgian linen jacket was getting inappropriately rumpled, and it was starting to look like she would be late to her own screening. Irrationally perhaps, but also viciously, she blamed Annabeth for all of this.

Annabeth, meanwhile, was obsessing over the placement of the new optical, her own version of the last-minute-anxiety fire drill. That Laura had been able to keep working without her the night before—even for the forty minutes it took her to drive to Venice, make a tuna sandwich, and drive back—had made her territorial and a little bit insane.

"It's five fucking frames!" Peter said at a quarter to three, as he watched her running the footage back and forth for what seemed like the twentieth time. Peter was the only human on the planet who could really judge what Annabeth had done—not just with the stupid dissolve but with the whole film. He was the only other person who had seen all the footage, knew all the changes, the only one who could comprehend what she had invented, what she had elegantly finessed, what she had left out because she had to. Unfortunately, she didn't care what Peter thought. She cared what Laura thought, and to a lesser extent Simpson, but also David. And where the hell was David? He'd promised to call when he woke up.

David was driving to Dr. Leight's office in the Palisades. He always felt better in the car than anywhere else. Being able to see so much of his surroundings while remaining sheltered and, to some extent, soundproofed in the mock room of the car's interior was like being present and absent at the same time; in the world but also out of it. It was how he imagined it would feel to be dead. He knew it was wrong to love driving as much as he did (fossil fuels, foreign oil, urban sprawl, all of it came down to driving too much), but it was his birthright as an Angeleno; he couldn't help himself.

Dr. Leight had been treating David since childhood. She had a sunny office full of contemporary art that reminded him of being happy and small. After examining his foot, she gave him a shot of antibiotics and told him to come in sooner next time and get a few stitches. Then she asked him if he knew the play *Philoctetes* by Sophocles.

"Philoctetes has this festering, wounded foot. It smells so bad, and he complains so bitterly, that Odysseus abandons him on a desert island."

"Are you saying I'm going to be abandoned?" he asked, hoping his tone was sufficiently arch.

"No, I'm telling you a story. So, after ten years, an oracle tells the Greeks that they need Philoctetes *and* his bow, which is magic, in order to win the Trojan War. To avoid getting shot on sight by this guy he's left to rot, Odysseus sends a young soldier who Philoctetes has never seen before to do the dirty work. He gives the kid a sob story to tell about how the Greeks have betrayed him too, so he can gain Philoctetes' trust and disarm him. And it works, up to a point. But Philoctetes is so pathetic, the kid falls apart—he admits it's all a trick and gives the old guy back his magic bow."

"Huh," said David. He had wanted to ask her for a prescription for Vicodin, but if he mentioned it now it would seem too intentional. She'd know what he was thinking. "Why did you tell me that?"

"Because it's a good story," she said. "And you have a festering foot injury. And no one seems to read it anymore."

"At least mine doesn't smell," said David.

"You'll be fine," she told him.

David nodded but suspected the story was supposed to mean more. The young man who has to do the dirty work of the big hero

Odysseus, weighed down by all that history and virtue the Greeks were so famous for. It was like all those dead fucking Jews he wasn't allowed to let down. Very clever, that Dr. Leight. She'd blocked his request for painkillers intentionally.

"Sorry, I didn't mean to lecture you," she said, then, seeing his consternation.

"Oh, no, it sounds worth reading," said David. "I bet my parents even have a copy. I'll check it out next time I'm over there." It amazed him how his social self could continue on autopilot while the edges of his mental frame were already turning so dark.

"Send them my regards," said Dr. Leight.

Annabeth managed to have a minor accident on the way to Long Beach—rear-ending a Lincoln that was crawling along at five miles an hour as she careened off the ramp from the 710. (The freeways had been empty and she had made up considerable time en route.) The Lincoln sustained very little damage but Annabeth, seatbeltless because of the heat, bruised her nose and breastbone on the steering wheel of her Civic and found that it hurt to breathe as she exchanged insurance information with the seventy-four-year-old Mrs. Myra Last, who was wearing orange lipstick and looked like a bent brown stick.

When Annabeth finally walked into the the auditorium it was five minutes after four, but the lights were still up. She found Laura standing in the back. The seats, just as predicted, were filled mostly by people who looked like they spent the majority of their waking hours playing golf. The marketing people were walking around making sure everyone had a response card and a stubby pencil with which to complete it.

"This is a disaster," whispered Laura.

"I know," said Annabeth. "I'm sorry. You were totally right."

Laura wanted to accept the apology, but she was too agitated. Then she noticed Annabeth's face, which was even paler than usual. "What the hell is wrong with *you*?"

"I had a car accident on the way over." Annabeth was shaking—a delayed reaction.

It took a moment for Laura to understand what she had just heard—the information had to fight its way past the obsessively detailed mental list of things-to-fix-next-time that she'd been keeping all afternoon. When it finally landed, Laura's anxiety changed its shape: what had been spiky and contained became formless and immense. "Well, I hope to hell nothing else goes wrong," she snapped over her shoulder, disguising the emotion in her voice. She half-ran to the ladies' room and locked herself in to the farthest stall. Then she sat, head on knees, until the sensation of being in a free-falling elevator abated. She did not want Annabeth to die in a car accident. She did not want to be left alone with this movie.

David arrived just as the lights were going down. He found Annabeth almost instinctively and took her hand in his. Relieved, she pulled him closer. She wasn't dead and neither was David and neither was Mrs. Last. She felt a strange rush of gratitude as the movie began.

The opening sequence (it didn't yet have credits over it) was a long tracking shot of Bunny walking along the side of a state highway at night. She was wearing a dress, a raincoat that was obviously not warm enough for the blustery weather, and pumps. Not hooker shoes, but not the sort of shoes anyone would choose to wear for a long walk on asphalt either. Laura said the scene told you everything you needed to know about Bunny. Annabeth had always been willing to admit that it was a beautiful piece of footage and that it certainly made you curious about the character but, since you never found out why she was walking on the highway, or saw her in the outfit again, or even knew—as those who had read the previous draft of the script did—that the highway was in Oklahoma, not far from Tulsa, where Bunny had come from but would never return, it seemed an unfair place to start. She had cut together the scene of Bunny on the highway so that it was exactly as Laura had designed it: funny, because her coat wouldn't stay closed and she wrestled with it in an almost slapstick dance; sad, because there is something intrinsically sad about a woman alone on a highway; and mysterious, because there was so much the audience just could not know. Seeing it on the big screen, she understood that Laura had been right. It really was the whole movie in one shot.

Laura didn't return from the bathroom until the end of reel 3. She sat on the aisle in the back row with Annabeth, David, and Simpson but said nothing and left as soon as the lights came up. There was something missing in her movie, something big, and she had no idea what it was. She should have invited Annabeth and Peter and Simpson out for drinks afterward and allowed them to convince her otherwise, but she went home to Greg instead, and lay beside him in silence while he watched television and held her hand.

———

When Annabeth and David got home that night, she made fierce love to him. She wanted to devour him—all his softness, all his maleness, all his intelligence and wit. She wanted to squirm out of her own skin and into his. David was surprised at first, but perfectly happy to be devoured. When they were done bucking and yelping, they looked at each other with strange curiosity: Is there someone else in there—inside that head, animating that body? Someone I haven't met yet? Do I love him? Do I like her?

Part 4

REVERSALS

22

The Long Beach audience was largely mystified by *Trouble Doll,*
and they hated Bunny. "Wimpy," "Airhead," "Not pretty enough
to be such a dope" were some of their comments. Laura refused
to read the burgeoning scroll of postscreening notes faxed by
Halo executives to the cutting room the next morning—she
wouldn't even let Annabeth tear them off the machine. Crouching next to the fax until her calves went to pins and needles,
Annabeth read them all, many of them twice. She recognized
the criticisms—they were of a piece with the comments she'd
made herself when she first read the script, as well as those
she'd muttered as she had macheted her way through her worst
days in the cutting room. Bunny was as inert as egg white, as

dull as soap. You kept wanting her to walk away, but she just wouldn't.

Simpson also read the notes, after finally tearing them off the machine. When he was finished reading, he called a meeting with Halo to discuss "solutions." It was the first time Annabeth had seen him in action, and she was impressed by his passion. The color came up in his cheeks. "What would that audience have thought about *Wild at Heart*?" he asked the telephone. "What would they have made of *sex, lies, and videotape*?"

While waiting for Laura and Simpson to return from the "solutions" meeting, Annabeth ran the movie twice at high speed. She went back to the notes from the set and the notes from dailies. She forced herself to imagine restoring long-abandoned sequences and to consider ordering reprints of alternate takes that no one had ever considered any good. She even reconsidered the sin of voice-over narration. (Adding narration in postproduction, Janusz had once said, was "like the shirt saying 'I'm wid sztupid,' " an editor's humiliating admission of total defeat.) What she didn't prepare herself for was what happened: Laura and Simpson returned with Halo's promise to back fifty thousand dollars' worth of additional photography.

"Reshoots?" Annabeth repeated, knowing she should have felt relieved.

"More is better," said Simpson, standing in the doorway.

"More is morphine," said Laura at his side. They were like the hipster version of *American Gothic,* Annabeth thought, hating them.

She hunched in her swivel chair, wondering why the idea of reshoots sounded so bad to her, waiting for the feeling of having been tricked to go away.

"Cheer up, Annabeth, we're in Schaefer City," Simpson said.

"Who's going to write them?" she asked him.

"Don't worry. Laura can do it. I'll even bring Ramona back for a few days to help stir the pot." He looked at Laura as he said this, open to her veto, but she just nodded. Annabeth wondered whether anyone was going to ask *her* to contribute to this mysterious new stew they were about to concoct.

"Go home," said Laura. "You deserve some time off. Go home and relax." But Annabeth knew she didn't really mean "relax," she just meant "get out of my way," and there was no way she was going to do any such thing. As soon as she left they were going to sit down and do exactly what she had been doing for the last three hours . . . without her. She was the only one of them who actually knew the movie completely—all the takes, all the shots. And she was the only one who could see past her own ego to the truth of how it played. Why was she suddenly, apparently, inessential? She looked to Simpson for help, but he just smiled and nodded.

"Well, I guess I'll call it a night then," she said. She stopped herself from volunteering to call Peter in to help them. If they hadn't thought of doing any "rewriting" tonight, with the film itself, she didn't want to suggest it. It was late, they would have to get tired soon anyway, and in the morning she would come in first thing and make another backup of the backup on Peter's system, just to be safe.

———

Annabeth drove off that night in a kind of trance. It was too early to go home—the house was empty, and so was the refrigerator. Instead, she followed the spindly bent parade of palm trees at the end of David's old street as though it led somewhere worth going. But it really didn't. As she found herself crossing the silent suburban neighborhood north of Montana Avenue, she thought of David's parents' house. He'd been spending a lot of time there lately—doing his laundry and retrieving old LPs was what he said, but it made her uncomfortable. She'd been invited there only once since Thanksgiving and only for a quick visit, not even dinner. David said they didn't really eat formal meals, but she knew that was a lie. When she'd said the words "Duluth, Minnesota" to Naomi the first time, the woman's face had closed up like a clam. But it was true that the eerie laboratory of the Bronsteins' kitchen didn't seem like a place where food was prepared. There were no burners on the stove, only glass with some kind of starburst pattern printed on it where the burners were supposed to be. And though the giant, double-doored refrigerator was fully stocked with groceries, they were all sealed in plastic containers announcing their provenance: Gelson's. Laura's groceries came from Gelson's, too.

On reaching the intersection with Sunset Boulevard, Annabeth turned left, heading for the Gelson's in the Palisades. She'd driven past it dozens of times but had never gone inside. Maybe she would see Jack Nicholson contemplatively tasting olives, as Linda Bronstein claimed to have done. Maybe she would spend a thousand dollars on groceries, as Peter claimed his mother did annually at Christmas. Maybe she would think of a way to fix the movie and be allowed in on the rewriting process, instead of being pushed aside like a secretary who was taking too long at the typewriter.

The first thing she noticed inside the supermarket was the smell. It was missing. The mixture of mild disinfectant, old lettuce, mouse droppings, and slightly decayed beef fat that was the same at the Mar Vista Vons as it had been at the Hooley in Duluth and the Randalls in Austin was not present. How did they do it? The light at Gelson's was whiter, too. Maybe not particularly flattering to people but good for green vegetables and somehow also per-suasively antiseptic. The store was nearly empty of people, but the produce department was full of wonders: lingonberries, goose-berries, kumquats, quinces! She wondered if there had been a Gelson's when Hollywood was the new home for all those Euro-pean refugees. She could picture Billy Wilder weeping sentimen-tally over the sight of long-lost gooseberries. She wished Laura were there with her, so she could make that observation out loud to someone who would get it. Instead, she bought wild strawber-ries: $6.99 for a half-pint. The checkout girl didn't even blink. As Annabeth drove home along the PCH, she ate them out of the box, and they tasted more like strawberries than anything she had ever tasted before—almost fake in their specificity. They lasted her as far as the light at Chautauqua.

The next morning, Annabeth returned to the cutting room. She had a million excuses for why, but she didn't need any of them, because Ramona was waiting for her in the lobby. "Laura said you'd show me the cut," she said without making eye contact, let alone saying hello. Annabeth had never had much patience for anorexics, especially those over the age of seventeen. If you were locked in a dungeon in your youth, she thought, get help, or at least revenge, but don't make everyone who meets you have to wonder what the nature and extent of your suffering has been. Nevertheless, Ramona's presence gave her a legitimate job to perform that day, and for that she was grateful.

She found Ramona a chair, set it up next to the Avid, dimmed the lights, drew the blinds, and tried not to flinch when the writer commanded her to pause or rewind, so she could take seemingly endless, furious notes. When the last scene faded out, Annabeth politely asked, "So what do you think?" but she did not actually want to know the answer.

"It's great," said Ramona, while giving the impression of someone doing integral calculus in her head.

"Does it look anything like you pictured it would?" This was a dumb question, possibly even a hostile one, but Annabeth suddenly felt the need to probe. "It must be so weird to see your own life turned into a movie—I mean, I know it's not exactly your life, but Laura said parts of it are kind of close—"

"I'm sorry, I'm really distracted," said Ramona. "Do you have a continuity I can have? To take with me?"

Which brought Annabeth up short. She should have offered the current chronological list of scenes to Ramona before they'd started, just as she would have done for the composer or the ADR editor or anyone else who came to work on the movie during post. Ramona, by asking for it now, was both pointing out Annabeth's gaffe and putting her in her place at the same time. Annabeth felt horrible, only it was too late to do anything but rustle around for a copy of the thing and apologize profusely, which she did, wishing all the while that when Ramona got home she would feel the need to consume a gallon of Häagen-Dazs.

When the writer had the continuity in her hands and had paged through it cursorily, she looked up at Annabeth and said, "I'm going to want some changes."

23

Kurt Cobain's death was first reported on a Friday. David had been half-expecting it ever since the overdose the month before, but he still felt jolted. The cliché—*but he had so much to live for*—was all he could think. Frances Bean wasn't even two. He called Annabeth but she was "in with Laura" and couldn't be disturbed, so he wound up talking to Peter. Though they hardly knew each other, on hearing the news Peter made a noise that sounded like all the air being let out of a pool toy and David felt that he understood. "Oh, man," Peter said, "that just sucks."

"I know," said David.

And they sat in silence for quite a while, until Peter finally said, "Thank you for telling me. I'm going to turn on the radio now," and they got off the phone.

———

By the time Annabeth got home that night, David was asleep. He was also asleep the next morning when she left the house, and so on through the weekend, and then, on Monday evening, Laura actually hired a masseuse to come and work on the cutting room staff, so it wasn't until Annabeth was listening to *Old Brown Show* late Tuesday night that she realized her boyfriend had lost someone truly important to him. She was listening in the dark, so it was almost like being in the room with him—or so she tried to convince herself.

"There are a lot of different reasons why people write songs, write letters . . . try and tell their stories," said David to his late-night listeners. "I think about this a lot because, well, maybe because I'm not much of a storyteller myself. I wish I was. Well, obviously, I'm talking to you now, and you don't even know me. Anyway, I've been thinking a lot about Kurt Cobain because the stories he told meant something to me, a lot more than most pop songs do, and I'm pretty sure I'm not alone on that one.

"You know, in some languages, the word *history* is the same as the word for *story.* It's just what we tell ourselves about why things happened the way they did, no matter what the scale of those things is. Because it's really the same thing, whether you're trying to communicate with your father, or your girlfriend, or your coworker, or the guy sitting next to you on the plane. You want to be seen and understood as you really are, not as anyone expects you to be."

Annabeth wondered whether she was the girlfriend in this sentence and, if so, what else she had failed to see and understand about David.

"Kurt's songs are all about that, about not really knowing who you're talking to, who the other person really is. The 'you' he's singing to is always in play and, instead of that making his songs seem unfocused, I think it makes them more interesting. I'll spare you my singing but there are tons of examples. And it's the way he was able to turn that inside out that makes him a more important songwriter than, like, Billy Corgan or Thurston Moore. It probably won't be obvious or come into focus for another dozen years, maybe longer, but the way he blurred the line between collective and individual is seminal. It's like the essence of what's wrong with my generation, with the country we live in, with everything now, really: We don't know where the intimate ends and the public begins. You know what I mean? The boundaries just keep moving."

Annabeth wasn't sure whether David was saying Cobain's songs were a symptom of this problem or a chronicle of it, but whatever he was saying, he sounded upset. He was talking loudly and very fast.

"I mean, for the sixties generation, it was like 'If you're not part of the solution, you're part of the problem.' Everything was clear. Like with Dylan, at first his 'you' is so clearly the other. You, who philosophize disgrace; you masters of war; you, clueless Mister Jones . . . And I'm sure that's why people felt so betrayed when he turned it around. You've got a lot of nerve, *How does it feel?* Suddenly, they were the problem."

He paused. It was slightly longer than a radio pause is supposed to be, but when he resumed his voice was calmer.

"We've replaced all that sincerity with irony now. And Kurt's the only one, for me, who really cuts through. Who tells the truth."

Annabeth had never heard David speak at such length or so seriously, not even about events in his own life. She could tell he was really just struggling to turn an emotional loss into something intellectual, something he could wrap his head around, and this made her feel for him because it was a trick she knew all too well.

But she also felt jealous. Those tangled thoughts should have been hers to hear first, and he had laid them out for all of late-night Los Angeles, as though he had no one else to talk to. And all she could do was tell him that she had listened and—if he admitted that anything was the matter at all—that she wanted to be there for him in the future. It didn't sound like nearly enough.

24

Laura was supposed to be spending her every waking hour in a suite at the Chateau Marmont with Ramona, working on the reshoots, but their relationship was no better than it had been before shooting started (and there was no longer the prospect of making a complete and perfect version of the movie in either of their heads to keep them amiable). One particularly listless morning she decided to drive over to the cutting room and check in on Annabeth and Peter, who were essentially getting paid to wait, which killed her. Because her contract was an over-scale lump sum, every extra week just came out of that figure, whereas members of the editors local got paid for every hour they worked.

"Let's go get some sushi," she said to them both when she got there, but Peter had a dentist's appointment and had to decline.

"My car or yours?" said Annabeth.

"Here's a really crazy idea," said Laura. "Let's walk." It was only about a mile, after all, and the weather was mild enough. But once they were out and about among the silent little-box houses of Nebraska Avenue, walking seemed so very peculiar that they looked at each other and had to laugh.

"It's like we're the last people on earth," Annabeth said.

"God, do you think there are gamma rays or something we don't know about? Is it safe?" Without even thinking, Laura pronounced the last three words in Laurence Olivier's Nazi accent from *Marathon Man. Iz et seff?*

"Yes, it's safe, it's very safe, it's so safe it's unbelievable!" Annabeth said back, which was the spirit if not the letter of Dustin Hoffman's response.

"Thus far I find you rather repulsive; may I say that without hurting your feelings?" rejoined Laura, which was another line from the movie and made them laugh some more. Everything was funny, all of a sudden. Especially to Laura, who was stoned.

Once inside the tiny restaurant, Laura became almost immediately engrossed by the television mounted on the wall above them: a high-speed car chase was taking place in Asuza with a news helicopter along for the ride. "When did this become the news? Metal and concrete, cars chasing cars chasing cars . . . it's *so boring.*"

"At least the sound is off," said Annabeth, trying to get into Laura's groove.

"They still need a cutaway."

"Totally," Annabeth agreed. "Insert on the perp's face, point of view from the street, something."

"Insert on uni," said Laura, looking at her dish and giggling. The food looked like butterscotch custard to Annabeth, but she suspected it was something inedible. She had opted for the miso soup and was avoiding the slimy seaweed as best she could.

"Do you ever listen to that show on KROQ? The one with Dr. Drew?" she asked Laura. It was not such a long leap from the car chase to *LoveLine*—both belonged to the slow-motion-train-wreck class of entertainment.

"That show where some kid is always asking if he can get AIDS from fucking the family dog?"

Annabeth nodded. "I just remembered this caller I heard once, at the beginning of the movie. He sounded so familiar."

For a moment, Laura looked startled. "Like someone on the movie?"

"I don't think so. He had this affected way of talking, like he was too much of a gentleman to say 'blow job' but circumstances were forcing him to be indelicate."

Laura shrugged and dispatched the rest of her sea urchin, her eyes wandering back toward the TV.

"So, like, he'd go out to buy a newspaper or something and wind up with a streetwalker underneath the 101, or he'd get the girl from the espresso place to go with him to Griffith Park on her break . . . He had a bunch of examples . . ." This story had somehow seemed like an amusing anecdote before she'd started talking, but now it just sounded gross and she didn't know why she was telling it. She forged on anyway, hoping to bump into whatever had struck her as amusing at first. "Dr. Drew said it was an illness, like alcoholism—and that it was usually as much about getting found out and punished as about the sex—and the guy said, 'Yeah, tell that to the president.'" There'd been another headline about the Paula Jones thing earlier in the week. Maybe she'd seen something about that on the sushi bar TV without realizing it.

The chef placed Annabeth's bamboo pallet of California rolls in front of her, then a large ceramic bowl of sashimi in front of Laura.

Laura looked down at her watch. It had been a gift from Greg—an apology. He couldn't possibly have called *LoveLine*—he had some shame, after all. But he'd said the same thing about Clinton to her the other day, more or less.

"Goatish behavior," she said to Annabeth, echoing Hugh Grant's public apology for getting a blow job on Hollywood Boulevard, though she could see that the reference was lost on Little Miss Milkmaid from Minnesota. She didn't know what she was talking about; she'd just blundered onto the subject the way she blundered into everything else: trial and error and an uncanny instinct for the location of other people's buttons.

Looking at Laura's profile in the contrasty afternoon light, Annabeth could see that she was irritated. Her bowl was still full of fish but she was making the silent scribbling gesture that meant *Check, please.*

"So, back to the coal mine?" she said to Annabeth.

Laura returned to the Chateau Marmont with a gathering sense of purpose that afternoon. She'd never thought of herself as much of a writer, but that was mainly because she sucked so badly at dialogue. While driving back across town it had come to her that the work they needed to do on Bunny's character was not about speeches at all.

"This really isn't working," she told Ramona when she got back to the bungalow.

"What isn't?"

"This," said Laura, gesturing haphazardly at the space between them. "You and me writing together. Don't you agree?"

"It's funny you should say that because I finally did something good today, while you were gone. I was just about to print it out," said Ramona, turning back to the computer and placing her hand on the mouse.

"You're just too close to it all, is the thing," Laura went on, having prepared her remarks in advance. "I'm not talking about the screen credit or anything, but I just—I want to do the rest of this by myself."

Ramona stopped mousing. She tried to keep herself from saying what came to her lips, but quickly gave up. "How did you get to be *such* a cunt?"

"Excuse me?"

"You heard me. Who the fuck do you think you are?"

"There's no reason to go crazy," said Laura.

"I'm not crazy, I'm angry. There's a difference. And I have every right to be angry because you're standing there screwing me." With deliberate gestures, Ramona dragged a folder across the screen and trashed it, making sure to also empty the trash. "So fuck you!" she said and, stopping long enough to grab her shoulder bag and sunglasses, she walked past Laura and out the door.

Laura could see that Ramona had done something on the

computer and she had a feeling she knew what that something was, but she really, truly didn't care. The work they'd done together was crap. She had a different idea about Bunny now, and it was finally crystal clear in her mind: Bunny was funny and sad at the same time, like Giulietta Masina dancing her crazy mambo in *Nights of Cabiria,* like Lisa Eichhorn getting her vodka bottle back from Jeff Bridges in *Cutter's Way,* like Annabeth getting all weepy over the ridiculous sculptures at the La Brea Tar Pits. Bunny was Annabeth.

"No great loss there," said Simpson the next day when Laura told him about her schism with Ramona. "Too bad it doesn't save us any money."

"If you want to save money, why don't you just get rid of Annabeth?"

"Really?"

They were sitting at a table within spitting distance of the giant copper vat of beer at the restaurant across from the cutting room. Laura had invited Simpson "to talk about Bunny," but she didn't really want his advice; she just wanted him to think she did.

"I think Peter can cut in the reshoots, with my help. He's a smart kid. Besides, it's going to be really simple. I just want to fill in some of Bunny's childhood."

Simpson nodded and focused on preparing a very complete bite of all the foods on his plate—a little bit of grilled fish, some watercress, a touch of garlic aioli. "I don't think a few weeks of Annabeth's salary is going to stretch fifty grand into a budget for period cars and wardrobe. Do you?"

"No, that's not what I'm talking about. I'm just going to shoot everything super-tight, as though the frame itself is the limitation of memory. Do you know what I mean? So we won't have to dress extras or anything but it will also be really interesting visually. I mean, enough already with the flashed-film-stock, bleach-bypass look. Wouldn't it be cool to do something new?"

While Simpson finished his meal with great precision, Laura explained her ideas in general terms, suggesting the sorts of locations she pictured using and the scenes she planned to shoot.

Simpson liked the new concept immensely. It was not only smart and stylish but would be cheap. The suggestion about firing Annabeth came back to him only the next morning, while he was reviewing the latest cost summaries.

25

Annabeth next crossed paths with Simpson in the parking lot as she was arriving for work. There was still nothing for her to do in the cutting room, but Laura had been writing furiously and Annabeth was hoping she would ask her to read the new scenes as soon as they were ready, so she kept showing up, being patient, batting away doubts like flies.

"Hey!" Simpson called out to her, waving cheerily and beckoning. She went toward him, of course. "Laura tells me you're leaving us," he said. "Please don't tell me you're doing Sharon Fried's picture at Propaganda!"

"Uh, no," said Annabeth as all of the blood in her body seemed to succumb to gravity. "It's personal," she added, which seemed undeniably true as soon as the words escaped her mouth. It had to be personal. Laura said she was leaving?

"Oh," said Simpson. "I'm sorry." He looked truly abashed, as though he assumed "personal" meant *death in the family* or *hospitalization for drug abuse.*

"It's okay," she said. And then she looked at her watch and said she had to go. Stunned, she went back to her car and sat inside it to collect her thoughts. What would she tell people? In a normal workplace, you could blame the boss, or the boss's cretinous son, or bean counters and number crunchers—a rare instance of a phrase she could recall hearing in her father's voice. But the only two authority figures in Annabeth's work life were Laura and Simpson, and she couldn't afford to bad-mouth either one of them. Moreover, she didn't want to.

She spent twenty minutes in the car imagining every bad thing Laura might say about her: she was lazy, she was deceptive, her behavior with Simpson was presumptuous, her sense of story was juvenile, her inability to give any consistent style or "edge" to the picture, inexcusable. But in the back of her mind Annabeth knew that she had washed up on a familiar shore and it had nothing to do with any of these potential criticisms. She put her fingers on the ignition key but didn't turn it. Instead, she left the car, stopped at the ladies' room to wash her face, and then forced herself back through the carpeted, fluorescent hallways to the cutting room, her cutting room. There, as she had half-expected, she found Laura already seated at the Avid, hard at work. She was watching Bunny enter the party with the Chinese lanterns, the scene now complete with background wallah and jazzy underscore. Annabeth knew that Laura was aware of her presence as soon as the light from the open door fell across the screen, but she waited until the exchange of dialogue between Bunny and Jude was over to stop the playback. Bunny no longer said, "All I want is a chance."

"Look," Laura said, as she swiveled her chair, "it's about money. We let you go, and I can hire a crane for the reshoots. You know, you cost a lot with health and welfare. And I can really cut the rest myself . . ."

Annabeth nodded. She had not expected the money angle, but it told her that whatever else was going on, her departure was a done deal, irretrievable. "I'll leave things in good order," she mumbled, wishing fervently that Laura would feel sorry for her and relent. "You could keep me on and not pay me, you know," she said, her voice cracking.

Laura had been sitting with her legs splayed out straight from her chair, looking at her feet, but now she pulled them under her and picked up her head to look at Annabeth. "You know that would never work. You resent being my employee so much it's like there's a force field around you sometimes. The thing is, you *are* my employee, or you were. Anyway, I'm just tired of it."

Annabeth was stunned. Suddenly, she felt very uncomfortable standing in the doorway but, looking around, saw nowhere else to go. "I can't believe this," she said. "I can't believe you would do this to me."

"You'll get over it," said Laura. Her hands were shaking but her voice was calm.

26

The only person, besides David, who Annabeth told about losing her job was her old friend Denise. "I'm cursed," she said.

"Where's the curse? You'll still get the credit, won't you?"

"I guess."

"Annabeth, you have a union." Denise was always practical, which was a large part of why Annabeth felt it was safe to tell her about what had happened, but even though she could have anticipated most of what her old friend would say to her, she found it frustrating to get solutions instead of sympathy.

"Yeah, but she's going to blackball me."

"I thought you said it was about money. Did you actually do something wrong?"

It was a sincere question, asked without accusation, but Annabeth was amazed to hear it come out of her friend's mouth. She was speechless.

"Did you ever try going back to Al-Anon?" Denise said, after the silence had become uncomfortably long.

Annabeth's exasperation became audible in the form of a hissed breath. Getting fired from *Trouble Doll* was not anything she'd gotten herself into by making stupid choices. She didn't doubt that the children of alcoholics tended to be irresponsible or prone to addiction themselves, but she had been hardworking, and thorough, and loyal to the point of humiliation. "I don't see the connection," she said.

"I think you might, though—I mean, if you went. That whole thing of putting people on pedestals, especially these people you work with. And then they betray you and you get so abandoned and despairing. I mean, yeah, it's Hollywood, but it's also typical Al-Anon stuff and you don't have to be so alone with it."

The word *Hollywood* had once conjured so much. Annabeth recognized the freight of those illusions in Denise's comment—how could she understand? In Annabeth's Hollywood there were no klieg-lighted premieres among colossal sphinxes or cocktail parties held inside buildings shaped like derby hats. It was all different, and worse, and as impossible to explain as it was to conform to. She could taste the dry residue of the city air in the back of her throat. The telephone receiver felt hot and greasy and suddenly so heavy she wanted to throw it across the room.

"Annabeth?" said Denise, "Are you okay?"

"Yeah. I just never thought my life would be like this."

Annabeth remembered how blue the sky sometimes looked outside the window of her childhood bedroom, the color of Lake

Superior reflected back to her from the other side of the hill. She used to lie on her bed telling herself that something as beautiful as that blue would happen to her if she could just get out, get away.

"Yeah," said Denise, "I know. No one ever does."

After four months of steady employment, Annabeth had plenty of money in the bank, but her underlying sense of imminent poverty had kicked in as soon as the doors of Big Time had closed behind her. The days were unbearably long and she had no use whatsoever for David's companionship. She took herself to her first Los Angeles Al-Anon meeting mostly, she told herself, to get out of the house without having to spend any money. She chose the meeting at the Brentwood Presbyterian Church because she knew where it was, and because the recorded message told her there was a meeting there within a few hours of her decision to go, but also because she assumed that in that well-watered enclave she would be spared contact with the desperate types she imagined attending meetings in the church basements of Venice.

She got to the corner of Bundy and San Vicente five minutes before the meeting was supposed to begin but dawdled as she walked from the parking meter to the church. Once upstairs, she was surprised and relieved to find a folding chair at the end of the second-to-last row. No one even glanced in her direction as she sat down. The meeting came to order almost immediately, chaired by a mousy thirtyish woman with a nervous smile. During the preliminaries, she asked if there was anyone new present who wished to introduce themselves, but Annabeth pretended not to hear.

The meeting began in earnest with the twenty-minute testimony of an overweight white man in his forties who was wearing track pants and a T-shirt emblazoned with the name of a pharmaceutical product. At first, this outfit made Annabeth fear that he was crazy or homeless—the clothes looked like thrift-store finds—but as he continued to speak, it became apparent that he was in fact a physician of some sort. "In my line of work, you're *supposed* to think you're God," he said, which got a huge laugh from everyone but Annabeth.

"It never ceases to amaze me," he went on, "that I could get all this way, do all the things my mother always said she wanted me to do—the job, the marriage, the grandchildren—and still feel like a pathetic, fat little boy pleading with her to get off the couch and make dinner."

Ick, thought Annabeth, picturing this scene all too vividly taking place in the living room of her own childhood home, where her mother had certainly never passed out—Annabeth had never even seen anyone lying down there, at all, that she could remember. And then she recollected something she had long forgotten: sitting next to her father on that couch and watching *On the Waterfront* on television with the living room lights all turned off. She had been too young to follow the story of the movie, but so delighted to be alone with her dad that she had nestled into the couch cushions just to watch the expressions on his face. He had frowned and scowled and smiled and laughed and only turned to look at her once. *He must have realized I was too young to under-*

stand that movie, she thought, trying desperately to hold on to the image of her father's face looking at her with love and concern, but it was chased away by the enthusiastic applause following the fat physician's testimony.

She sat through the whole meeting feeling variously bored, annoyed, frightened, and trapped, but also fascinated. When a slight, darkly tanned woman told a convoluted story about a conflict with a coworker who had threatened to have her fired, Annabeth felt sure that the woman had really stolen her coworker's commission, in spite of all her talk of being a victim. A burly handsome man who wittily and insightfully described his difficulties with an apparently schizophrenic son began, toward the end of his four-minute "share," to seem to Annabeth like a manipulative bastard who forced his wife to make all the difficult decisions. This became a pattern as the meeting went on. She would start out thinking a person was normal enough but after three minutes realize that he or she was self-deluding, controlling, dishonest, or just pathetic—except in cases where that was what she thought of them in the first place. When the chairperson announced that the time for sharing was up, Annabeth was relieved to get away.

Driving home, she argued with herself about what she had just witnessed. Sure, she had some of the same feelings as the so-called Al-Anonics. Their sense of worthlessness, their unbearable anxiety, their certainty that they would screw everything up eventually and so why not just get it over with and at least have control of *that* much—this was all unpleasantly familiar. But there was also a self-indulgent, narcissistic quality in these people that she actively despised. The way they went on and on about their stupid injuries and paranoias, the way they let themselves complain and blame and whine was disgusting. Annabeth would never say the words "I almost lost everything!" as had a blond woman wearing an immense diamond ring. Annabeth had never *had* everything. She was pretty sure she'd never even wanted it. These people seemed to believe their special version of God liked them better than they liked themselves. Annabeth's God hated his own mistakes the same way she did, the way any sane person does, she thought.

Driving south on Lincoln Boulevard, she passed one of a chain of local stores called Smart & Final Iris. She'd passed it hundreds of times but had never been inside, despite wondering for ten years what a store with such a name might sell. She never saw the sign without thinking of the silent-film device that meant the story was over: the encroaching circle of blackness that swallowed what had come before. "Final iris" was a perfect description for this, and a final iris that was also "smart" made the featureless concrete box look like the perfect antidote to the roiling confusion of the Al-Anon meeting.

As it turned out, the place was a catering-supplies discount store, inexplicably named. She watched shoppers load up on immense canisters of Coffee-mate, stainless steel bowls as big as tractor-trailer tires, and rolls of plastic film sufficient to prepare a whole house for refrigeration, a whole life. Annabeth bought a gallon-sized measuring cup made of Pyrex for $4.99. It was the only thing in the store of monster-sized cookware that she could imagine being able to use.

27

One summer night in a parking garage in Century City, David asked Annabeth to marry him.

"Are you insane?" she asked back.

"Maybe," he said, "but that's not why I think we should get married."

They were in his car, seven or eight levels underneath the Avco theater, where they had gone to see a midnight show of *Natural Born Killers,* and they were stuck in traffic. It was far too soon after the Northridge quake to be creeping along at less than five miles an hour that far below street level, and David's offer had been an act of desperation, although a sincere one. The only way out would have been to abandon the car and walk home—obviously not an option—so they persisted in their glacial progress upward, feeling scared and foolish and mad at Oliver Stone, all at the same time.

Annabeth regretted her response the moment it left her mouth, but despite her regret she remained speechless, trapped in a state of tremendous anxiety and sorrow for which neither the movie nor the traffic jam were entirely to blame. "That came out wrong," she tried, finally. "I just don't understand how you could think that was a good question to ask at this particular moment."

Unfortunately, while she had been formulating this statement, David had begun to weep. It was a sight Annabeth could not bear. She averted her eyes, but the image was intractable. He turned on the radio in an attempt to provide cover, only there was no radio reception in the underground garage. Annabeth then foraged on the floor of the car for a cassette and came up with *In Utero*. But by the time their ticket had been read and the gate had swung up, she could tell she'd made a terrible error of some sort and ejected the tape. The radio was preset to KROQ—certainly *it* would be safe from tragedy at that hour on a Saturday night. Sure enough, it was broadcasting talk: a giggly actress was speaking about the party she'd been to earlier and entertaining the possibility that her skirt was too short. Stupid but harmless.

David steered the Aries out onto the Avenue of the Stars and followed it through the empty canyon of skyscrapers to the freeway entrance. Once they were enveloped by the relief of normal freeway speed, the mood in the car shifted enough for him to reclaim some dignity. He even laughed at the antics on the radio. They were almost home when a segment with a familiar call-in voice came on. They were listening to *LoveLine,* and it was a rerun.

"Doesn't that sound like Laura's husband?" said David.

"Greg?" said Annabeth, feeling suddenly sick. "How do you know what Greg sounds like?"

"I met him when I came by the cutting room for lunch, remember? He told me he listens to my show."

Annabeth returned her attention to the radio broadcast, becoming increasingly alarmed.

What does my wife think? She doesn't. All she thinks about is her work and what restaurant to go to, said the man called Paul. It was absolutely Greg. She remembered watching Laura's profile that afternoon in the sushi bar and she knew that Laura had made the connection then. Everything that had followed had really followed from that.

Annabeth couldn't sleep that night, or the next, or the one after. In the moments when she was able to get herself off the hamster wheel of self-flagellation about her behavior with Laura, it was only to recall the terrible look of shame and rejection on David's face as they crept through the parking structure. She tried to picture what it would have been like to be living by herself during this horrible moment in her life—she would have stayed in bed all day with the shades drawn, living on peanut butter and tuna fish, occasionally making her way out to that horrible Vons supermarket where everyone looked like an extra from a Fellini movie. She was eventually going to have to apologize, or something, but there seemed to be no right thing to say or right moment to try.

There are sometimes "famous" conversations in the early days of a relationship. Remarks that the partners mythologize and that come to represent something about their couplehood that they couldn't otherwise express. For Annabeth and David, it had been a conversation about the architectural decorations called ding-bats—the metal doodads one sees affixed to the front of the same kind of boxy L.A. apartment buildings that also often have names inscribed on them: "Debby Do," "Esplanade," "Quo Vadis." One day, Annabeth had said to David that the dingbats looked to her like "malignant hubcaps" and David had said "more like decorative gunshot wounds" and then they both had laughed so hard their cheeks ached. What was so hilarious about it was not just that it was possible to have formed an articulate opinion about these ridiculous things, but that David and Annabeth—the two lone Linnaeuses of dingbatdom—had managed to find each other and share their thoughts on the subject. Much later, it occurred to Annabeth that this was not the first time she had mistaken this kind of coincidence for true love.

Annabeth really had no idea how lost and desperate a gesture David's proposal had been. She had been so mired in her own drama that she had entirely stopped monitoring his. Or perhaps that was the invisible design of their relationship from the beginning: he watched her, she watched herself, no one watched him.

In spite of his radio show, or perhaps because of it, David had been struggling desperately since the earthquake. He remembered Greg's voice so distinctly because he remembered everything about Annabeth's world—he was memorizing it in the hope that he might annex it, somehow, as a way out of his own. If he could put names to all the faces and voices and key facts (Greg = Harvard, artist, eyelid tremor), Annabeth would not realize what a disaster he really was. His proposal of marriage was a bid to freeze their relationship, not to grow it. And her response had hurt him, but not because he perceived it as a personal rejection. He'd wept because by refusing him, she'd busted him. He would have to find another imaginary life to inhabit, and he was too exhausted to do so.

28

In the weeks that followed, Annabeth surrendered to her black mood. And in the midst of this came her thirty-fifth birthday. It seemed unbearable. David, helpless in the face of her depression, which looked to him nothing like his own, purchased her a healing treatment at a spa in Koreatown, the suggestion of one of the interns at the station.

Annabeth made her way there on a searingly brilliant Tuesday afternoon. At the front desk, potted palms cast shadows on the green marble counter, and Annabeth detected the faint smell of sulfur. At the towel window, a young woman handed her a towel, a robe, a pink shower cap, a pair of flip-flops, and a brass locker key and told her to change and wait by the pool. It occurred to Annabeth that this was probably what it would feel like to be sent to one's death in a seemingly beneficent totalitarian society. On the way to her locker she stopped in the bathroom, where the water in the toilet bowl was so warm it felt like breath on her buttocks when she sat down. The banal office building was, in fact, built on top of a thermal spring.

In the pool area, where rock formations built out of spray-on concrete had gained a plausibly ancient patina, there were two pools: one large and hot, the other small and cold. When Annabeth entered the room in her scratchy white bathrobe, she saw a slight, dark-haired woman, quite naked, at the far side of the hot one. The woman sauntered through the thigh-deep water and then crouched, submerging herself to the shoulders and gazing implacably past Annabeth. She didn't really look like Laura, but the sight of her had nevertheless stopped Annabeth's heart. Lately, she could picture Laura's face only in two of its myriad moods, skeptical intensity or annoyed disinterest, but it was like tonguing the site of a missing tooth; she couldn't leave the hurt alone for long. And every time she launched a memory, she told herself that this time she would simply choose to end it differently, at least in fantasy. The blond woman at the Al-Anon meeting said she'd wasted half her life "waiting for the past to change," but this was different. Annabeth just needed to relocate the sense of promise she had felt so profoundly before things began to go wrong.

When her moment of panic had passed, Annabeth trod the rubber safety matting to the hot pool's edge and stuck her toes in the water. A few orange traffic cones were scattered about to prevent mishap, but other than herself and the crouching woman, the gymnasium-sized room was empty. She was shyly hanging her bathrobe on a poolside hook when she heard an approximation of her name called: "Annbeth?" A very beautiful young Korean woman dressed in highly unflattering black underwear was beckoning from the other side of the pool. She made a hand gesture that indicated that Annabeth should leave her robe behind.

So, naked except for her flip-flops, Annabeth followed the woman into the next room. It looked like a greenhouse, with long tables topped by shiny blue polyurethane pads that resembled pool toys. The woman patted one of these and Annabeth hopped up onto it, lay down, and soon felt a cold washcloth draped over her eyes. Then, several buckets full of warm water splashed over the length of her body. The woman scrubbed Annabeth's calves and feet with long strokes, her scourge lubricated with something cool and cucumber-scented. Crumbs of dead skin, sebum, lymph, and God knew what else rolled off her by the handful. Her scalp was scraped, her ears were purged, the space between each individual toe freed of any loose cell. For sixty minutes, she was made new.

Returned to the blinding brightness of the parking lot after this experience, Annabeth felt raw—she was still unused to being outside in the bright center of the day. As she drove between giant hedges, feeling clean and empty, she did something like praying—fervent wishing that the momentary sense of lightness she felt would last beyond La Brea Boulevard, would become something she could mentally re-create inside the dark house on Nowita Court. She found herself driving aimlessly, avoiding going home, and being flooded anew by memories of the "before" phase of her friendship with Laura.

———

After meeting Laura at the party with the elephant, Annabeth had wound up staying there much longer than she had expected to. She hadn't wanted to tag along too overtly, so she'd made a hapless tour of other rooms and drunk another plastic cup of wine before returning to the patio. She then found Laura dangling her legs in the neon-blue water at the shallow end of the pool, surrounded by avid young men—Laura was not giggling or splashing or tossing her hair but holding forth, and they were listening to her. Annabeth inserted herself beside a young man in a bowling shirt to listen to what later turned out to be one of Laura's set pieces, her theory of why the movie *Chinatown* was so universally revered in Hollywood.

"There isn't a starlet or a von Stroheim anywhere in the picture, and it takes place smack in the middle of the studio system's golden age."

Her listeners nodded thoughtfully, trying unsuccessfully to recollect an exception.

"Instead, it's all about water. And, like, water at the most elemental level: desert or torrent. It makes the movie business look so insignificant. Like, 'O look upon my works, ye moguls, and despair!' "

The young men—screenwriters and/or actors, Annabeth figured—smirked, shaking their heads. "We love *Chinatown* because we're self-loathing? Is that what you're telling me?" said one of them.

"Well, it's certainly a movie about America's love-hate relationship with wealth. I mean, Gittes is seduced by Mrs. Mulwray's class, right? She comes from the world of private clubs and goldfish ponds and then it turns out she's completely and utterly tainted. That's just the immigrant-outsider experience any way you look at it," said Laura. "Setting it in the movie business would have just been too on the nose."

Annabeth remembered watching as the young men drank their beers, smoked their cigarettes, or flicked their fingers in the pool. Did they recognize the extent to which they were all now standing in the same corrupted desert as Gittes, and Towne, and the malevolent Mulwrays? In any case, Laura had shut them up. Then Laura had smiled at Annabeth and shrugged. *Nothing to it,* she seemed to say, *just a party trick. Stick around and I'll show you another.* And Annabeth had. That had been the moment when she decided that Laura would be the one to move her life along to its next stage. And she'd believed that the look they had traded then had been mutual and well understood.

Passing the seven-story face of Kim Basinger on a billboard at the intersection of Pico and Crescent Heights, Annabeth was reminded of the day, sometime before the Oscars, when Laura had closed the cutting room door behind her and, in a state of breathless enthusiasm, announced that she had just had lunch with the guy she called her liar.

Laura had not only asked Annabeth to lie to Simpson about her lunch date that day, she'd told her about the conversation she'd witnessed between Golden and an A-list director they'd run into at the restaurant—"the sockless wonder," she called him. The two men had begun talking about the outrageous demands and pathetic antics of an actress they had both recently worked with, referring to her, consistently, as "the cunt," and Laura had mimicked them, seeming to enjoy herself immensely, relishing their easy contempt for the beautiful woman. Annabeth could remember sitting there at the Avid, knowing she was supposed to be enjoying this piece of gossip but instead feeling soiled by it. It was not that she was shocked by the word itself. It was Laura's ready adoption of it that surprised her, and the way she had taken it up against this other woman she obviously didn't even know on the say-so of these guys, who she *did* know but didn't seem to particularly respect. Annabeth had been so desperately attuned to her new boss, she hadn't had the nerve to say, "Enough," or even to frown or feign disinterest. And ever since then, in her own mind, she found that she could no longer think of the actress as anything other than "the cunt," a name she would not have called her worst enemy.

A Los Angeles County sheriff's car traveling in front of her made her think of the drive back from Manzanar. "My father disappeared when I was twelve," Annabeth had announced that day, as they passed the sign announcing their return to Los Angeles County. They were words she had never before said out loud, and she half-expected to be struck dead for saying them.

"I didn't know that," Laura replied. Her eyes never left the road, but Annabeth kept on talking.

"It wasn't the first time. I never knew what made him go. I never heard him complain or even saw him get angry, actually. Sometimes my mother yelled at him, but he would just sit there and take it.

"The only time I remember vividly was in the car. It was

winter—really cold, even in the car, and snow everywhere. I was in the back seat—my brother wasn't there for some reason. Anyway, Mom was giving Dad hell. About the bills that she'd been unable to pay when he was gone, and the lies she'd had to make up to cover for him at church and with her friends . . . She was yelling so hard that there was spit falling on the arm of her winter coat. I wanted to hide in the footwell—curl up like an armadillo behind my father's seat—but I didn't fit. Anyway, he stopped the car in the middle of nowhere. Just pulled over to the side. Then he got out and started walking. Maybe he was even running— I feel like I can see that, him running away in the snow in his Sunday suit. We were outside of town somewhere. Going to a wedding or a funeral? I can't remember. He didn't say anything; he just went."

"What happened?" asked Laura.

"What do you mean?"

"Did he come back? Did your mother slide over and start driving? Did you go on to the wedding or whatever without him?"

"I don't know," said Annabeth, shaking her head. "That's the whole memory: him walking away, my mother's spittle, me freezing my ass off in the back seat because he left the door open."

"You never knew where he went?"

Annabeth shook her head. "When he came back, we never asked. It seemed too risky. 'Don't buy into it,' my mother used to say. 'A mystery is just a secret no one is in on.' That always sounded so smart to me, but when you think about it, it doesn't really mean anything, does it?"

"Yeah, but you remember it," said Laura.

———

When Annabeth finally got home from her trip to Koreatown, she found David sitting on the couch, reading one of her old textbooks from film school. She'd taken them out as a way of asking herself if she was going to keep cutting or pack it in, but leaving them on the living room floor was as far as she'd gotten.

"Look," he said as she walked in, "is that the machine from your dream?" He turned the book toward her and pointed at a photograph of an editor operating an upright Moviola, circa 1949. It was a picture that had made a big impression on Annabeth the first time she'd seen it because the editor in the picture was wearing heels and a smart suit. She'd made moving to Los Angeles seem plausible, at one time in Annabeth's life. She had never looked all that closely at the machine in the picture because it was the same as the ones at school. But, sitting down beside David to gaze at it now, she saw that he was right. It was the machine in her nightmares.

"I haven't had that dream since I left the movie," she said. The words "got fired" still stuck in her throat.

"But that's really it?"

Annabeth nodded. He hugged her, he was so pleased with himself, but she broke the embrace.

"It still doesn't really explain anything if I don't know what the elephant is. The elephant in the room?" She tried again, free-associating: "A woolly mammoth? Mastodon? The McGuffin?"

"What is that, exactly, the McGuffin?"

"It's Hitchcock's term," she told him. "It's what he called the thing that everyone's after: the microfilm, the Maltese falcon, the intercostal clavicle . . . the point is, it doesn't matter what it actually is, it's a red herring."

"Does that explain your dream then?"

"How?"

"Well, the elephant in the room and the McGuffin are sort of the same thing then. The thing you can't identify too closely, that you agree to accept and ignore. So if your machine is an editing machine, it seems like the elephant is, like, the script, or the story, or the film itself."

"So why's it bleeding?"

"I don't know. Because you're afraid you're hurting it?"

She had a tremendous urge to hit him but restrained herself. She could tell from the look on his face that he wasn't sure whether what he'd just said even made any sense.

29

David and Annabeth held hands during the first half hour of *Trouble Doll*, which they went to see on opening day at the Laemmle Grand, downtown, one of two places in the city that it was playing. As Laura had feared, Halo was more or less dumping the film because its people had no idea how to market it. But they were still giving it a few weeks at the art theaters in New York and L.A. to see if it could build some word of mouth.

Settling in before the film started, Annabeth looked carefully and furtively at the other patrons—there were only a half dozen or so. What else did she expect at two P.M. on a Friday? Still, she found herself bristling. *She* would have come out to see this movie in the first week, even if she hadn't worked on it. David stroked her arm. "It's always like this here," he whispered. She nodded, focused on the screen as the theater was darkening, and then, seeing (of course!) that there would first be trailers, she turned to look quizzically at her boyfriend. He kept his eyes on the screen but felt her inquiry. "I used to come here sometimes," he whispered, "when you were at work."

The first trailer advertised a French film—the actors all looked familiar, but Annabeth couldn't name them. She pictured David sitting there alone, and wondered what else she didn't know about his life during the months when she'd thought about nothing but *Trouble Doll*. Then, a few rows behind them, an older woman asked her companion, "Have you ever been to the Dordogne?" in a loud voice. Annabeth's head whipped around to glare at the woman. People who talked in movies were intolerable to her.

When the second trailer started up, she was fascinated to see Gary Oldman portraying Ludwig van Beethoven. The narration explained that Ludwig van had enjoyed *a secret love the world has never known*.

"Strudel!" whispered Annabeth.

"I think it was kreplach," countered David. The women behind them hushed them aggressively and in unison, and Annabeth would have apologized but she heard the sad mandolin music that opened *Trouble Doll* and her mouth went dry.

The main titles were still played over Bunny, walking alone on the highway at night. Annabeth had cut it early in the schedule but had never seen the credits placed. Her own card appeared superimposed on the purplish blue of the evening sky; Laura's directing credit appeared against the shimmering lamé of the stripper's torso, the image that began the first scene.

For the rest of reel 1, Annabeth found herself unable to stay with the story. She kept feeling the need to concoct a defense for why Laura might have undone her work on the following scene, or the next, or the next. (She'd been premenstrual when she was working on that one; Laura had never liked that angle; the music cue just didn't fit the best take; and on and on.) But as the film unspooled, Annabeth's work continued to play out unaltered. The first thirty minutes was, cut for cut, exactly as she had left it.

Gradually and cautiously, she began to feel proud of her work: that was a nice elision there; good pacing in the driving sequence; elegant transition from Bunny's hands at the end of the fight scene to the money on the table in the next shot . . . She had forgotten all about the prospect of the reshoots by time the first new scene made its appearance. It was a flashback in which a towheaded child, obviously meant to be Bunny, sat in the back seat of a car as a snowy road unwound behind her. There was no voice-over, just a gradual sharpening of muffled dialogue from the front seat—a child's perception of a burgeoning argument between parents. The shot stayed tight on the little girl's face.

Annabeth was relieved that Laura had had the good taste to keep it there, on the girl, and not track off into the vagaries of the parental squabble. The only other shot in the sequence—if fifteen seconds of film could be called that—was a quick reverse from the girl's viewpoint as the car's driver, the dad, walked off into the snow, leaving his door open. The sound of the wind made it clear that it was extremely cold outside, and this detail jarred Annabeth into recognizing what she had resisted up till then: this moment in Bunny's fictional past was taken from Annabeth's real one.

This scene in the snow was the first of Laura's larcenies, but not the last. Other shreds of Annabeth's past were soon projected, elaborated, distorted, dramatized: the rolled-up mattress in the basement, the embarrassed yank of her mother's hand to avoid crossing the path of a creditor, the sighting of a man in a downtown alley who seemed at first to be her father but was only an old wino. Laura had assigned Annabeth's memories to a character who grew up to be a runaway, a stripper, and ultimately an anonymous corpse.

As the end titles began to roll, David could tell from Annabeth's posture that something was wrong. Ordinarily, she would sit quietly until she saw the Panavision logo, but now she seemed ready to leave before the crawl of actors' names had even finished.

" 'A film by Laura Katz,' " he whispered derisively. "I mean, who's it supposed to fool—her mother?" Of course, Annabeth had been the one who'd taught him to recognize the possessory credit as problematic in the first place, but now she found his comment embarassingly naïve. The credit was so beside the point.

30

Annabeth didn't remember the walk from the theater back to the car, and she didn't remember what words she had used to explain what she had just seen to David. They drove west on Sunset in silence, past Les Frères Taix and the Bright Spot, the Tropical bakery and Millie's, all places Annabeth used to meet her friends when she was new in town and everyone lived in Echo Park or Silver Lake—places so down-market that Laura had probably never set foot in any of them.

"You never told me any of those stories," said David.

Although she knew which stories he meant and he was right, *You're right* seemed like the wrong answer. "I must have told you some of them," she said. "Maybe you just weren't listening."

David was silent, but she could tell she had made him angry. He listened to everything she told him, and she knew that. He seemed to remember everything she told him, too. She looked out the window at a corner hamburger stand clad in greenish-gold glazed bricks. Their color grabbed the afternoon light and reflected it back in a weirdly brilliant flash. Even Tommy's Burgers is braver than I am, she thought.

"I didn't tell her those things because I trusted her, or loved her, or whatever it is that makes you think it really matters."

"Explain that to me?"

But she couldn't, really. "Well, I never told her about my dreams," she said, meaning the nightmares about the elephant. David misunderstood, thinking she meant her dreams of becoming Dede Allen or whatever—her movie-business dreams, which to him seemed highly impersonal, not to mention irrelevant.

"I told her that stuff because I wanted her to feel sorry for me," Annabeth said finally.

"Didn't work, did it?" David regretted the cruelty of this remark only slightly as he turned onto Highland Avenue.

"Where are you going?" asked Annabeth, but she knew.

Greg answered the door. He didn't look at her with any particular curiosity or emotion. "She's upstairs getting ready," he said, after raising his eyebrows to acknowledge the unlikelihood of the visit. Of course there was going to be a party, Annabeth realized, amazed that it had not occurred to her earlier. A party to celebrate the movie, to which she had somehow not been invited. She followed Greg inside and sat down on the gray-green couch. It faced a canyon view, and the golden light was tracing the ridges and rooftops as it receded. She had left David in the car, but now she wished he had come with her.

Laura entered the room wearing her bathrobe and with her face only partly made up, but she seemed both pleased and concerned to see Annabeth. Annabeth saw the *Did somebody die?* look on her face and found herself wanting to reassure, to make okay everything that wasn't. "Can you sit down?" she said.

Laura perched herself on the arm of a chair beside the sofa, modestly rewrapping her robe but keeping her eyes on Annabeth. "I would have invited you tonight, I just . . ." She trailed off, then changed her tack: "Simpson's been asking for you."

"I don't care about the party," Annabeth began. "I just came from the movie and I saw what you did. It fucking sucks, Laura." This speech had sounded fine in her head in the car—legitimately and justifiably outraged.

"What does?" Laura seemed genuinely uncertain.

"You stole my life."

Laura thought for a second, then nodded. "The reshoots, yeah, well, not really, but I guess I know what you're thinking."

"I'm not 'thinking,' I know it. It's the case."

Laura pursed her lips, looking speculatively at Annabeth.

"That scene in the snow? I've never told *anyone* about that before—not even David."

"Lots of families have fights in cars, Annabeth."

"Not like that one."

"No one could possibly think that but you."

"My mother will."

Laura scowled. "I hate to slag my own work, but this movie will be lucky to get to Wherever-the-hell-it-is, Minnesota, on video. Your mother is never going to see it."

"But my father might . . . and my brother."

"Look, Annabeth, I'm sorry you're upset, but I need to get dressed. Can we talk about this later?"

"I don't think you understand what I'm saying, Laura. I'm calling you a thief."

Laura stood up to go, hesitating only slightly at the vehemence of Annabeth's last remark. "Call me anything you want," she said after a moment. "I didn't see you doing anything with that stuff, I mean, besides trying to get me to think you were pitiful somehow—"

"What do you mean, 'doing anything with it'?"

"—which I don't and never will."

"It's my life—I don't have to *do* anything with it!"

Laura waited a beat, hoping Annabeth would hear what she'd just said. But Annabeth just sat there, teetering on the verge of tears. "Look, here's the thing. You're not an artist," Laura told her, "you're a craftsperson—a very talented craftsperson. But it's not the same thing. This is what artists *do*."

"What do you mean I wasn't doing anything with it?" Annabeth repeated. Her face was so red she felt that it might melt and slide off—and she was yelling. She never yelled. "Don't you have secrets you'd rather not see in a movie? Parts of your life you wouldn't want to share?"

Laura shrugged. "I don't share them then, do I?"

Annabeth swallowed. She wanted to point out all the things

she knew about Laura that she could tell the world if she wanted to, but even the whole thing about Greg and the radio was dubious. She'd never even had the nerve to ask what the deal was with Laura's ethnicity, which parent was Asian, if she was really Jewish, anything. And lying about her age was hardly shameful.

While she was trying to come up with a response, Laura turned and went upstairs.

On the ride home, Annabeth thought David was driving erratically. She felt like a turtle without its shell and, moreover, like the guy driving the shell wanted to kill her. As they merged onto the 101 South, she saw that her hands were clenched. She wanted to tell him what had happened at Laura's, but she still wasn't sure herself. Laura's remarks had stung as much as the insults her mother had sometimes flung at her: worthless, ridiculous, a fool. "She said I wasn't an artist," said Annabeth.

It might have been the worst thing a person could say, in their warped little corner of the universe. People like them didn't live in Los Angeles for the weather, after all; they came because they believed in the transformative power of an individual vision. It was preposterous but it was the whole point, even for David. The entertainment business was the only hope they had of ever participating, of belonging, of being in on the joke. He'd always thought that Annabeth understood the irony of wanting all that from a bloated, corrupt profiteering *business*, but the more she talked about her sense of having been lied to and stolen from, the more he realized she had actually bought into the fantasy of Hollywood the way that only an out-of-towner really could.

It was dark by the time they got there, but in the last mile or so of the Santa Monica Freeway, Annabeth caught sight of the tall palm trees at the end of David's former street. Silhouetted against the almost metallic blue of the early-evening sky, they still looked enchanted to her. "Prove me wrong," she'd told him that night—but she'd done her own proving.

She made a decision, that night, to go home—all the way home to Duluth. There was nothing rational about this decision, but there was very little left that was rational about Annabeth at that point. She'd spent most of the drive back from Laura's staring at David's rubber-thong-clad feet and wondering how she had ever convinced herself that sleeping with him was a good idea. No one in her family had feet like that. Her own feet were bony and attenuated, with high arches and long second toes—aristocratic, her father had told her once. David's feet were crude. What kind of grown man paraded around in flip-flops?

The next morning, she woke up at five and crept into the living room to call Northwest and book a flight. David was asleep, but gradually he became aware of Annabeth quietly opening drawers and rustling in closets in search of warm clothes. She answered his questions in monosyllables, and it wasn't until he asked whether she had a reservation and heard her say, "At noon" that he began to argue in earnest.

"I don't understand. You hate it there. What are you going to do all day?"

"I need to figure things out."

"In northern Minnesota, in October?"

"You wouldn't understand."

"Why not?"

The answer was because he had never left home himself, but she didn't say it. She didn't have to.

Part 5

WINTER

31

It was her first trip home in seven years and, as she probably should have anticipated, the house on Basswood Avenue seemed much smaller when she saw it. This was both because of the usual reverse-telescope perspective of time and because so many new houses had appeared in its vicinity. When Annabeth was growing up, their house had been at the edge of town, surrounded by woodland. ShopKo had first arrived in the neighborhood while she was away at college; most of the subdivisions were newer than that. She couldn't imagine who lived in them, but they seemed to contain families, and Annabeth felt a pang over this. Would her own childhood have seemed pleasant if there had been other kids around? Maybe. On the other hand, the presence of "normal" neighbors might have been all the more isolating.

What could she possibly have had in common with the kids who lived in those monstrosities?

"The McMansions," said her mother, noticing how Annabeth was craning her neck. "Didn't I tell you about them?"

"Maybe. When?" She was still wondering how on earth her mother had adopted the term *McMansions,* which—with McEverythingelse—had crossed over from hiphop slang to generalized hipster use only fairly recently in Annabeth's world.

"About three years ago, I guess."

"Are they nice?" She meant the inhabitants. Her mother understood this.

"Nice enough," said Eva, pulling up the gravel driveway in front of the squat, white clapboard house that, to her daughter, seemed to be screaming, "Paint me!"

"I'll get the bag," said Annabeth as her mother popped the trunk.

She'd flown into Minneapolis to get the cheaper fare, but the trade-off had been a four-hour drive home in which she'd found that she barely recognized her mother. Eva was just sixty, with a burnished, cheekbony face more Finn than Swede; her eye sockets and midsection were the only parts of her that seemed to show her age. Meanwhile her interests, the names of her friends, and even her taste in clothing were barely recognizable. She was wearing Levi's! The dour tax preparer of Annabeth's youth had become a cosmopolitan-looking retiree who said "McMansions," had taken ceramics, and kept in her ancient blue Volvo a stainless steel coffee thermos of the sort sold by Starbucks.

They entered the house through the kitchen—as everyone al-

ways had—and though there was nothing in the oven, the air still
smelled faintly of pot roast and onions, and marzipan, with just
the slightest undertone of sour drain. In the wake of those smells,
an army of memories marched into Annabeth's heart and started
jabbing vigorously with their bayonets. There were so many, and
they were so jumbled, that she could barely distinguish between
dinnertime quarrels (overwhelming tone: rancor) and Sunday
morning silences (surprising safety and warmth). The African vi-
olets on the windowsill reminded her of every sink full of dishes
she had used as an excuse to stay out of the dining room. The astounding persistence of the ancient Norge refrigerator, with its
rounded edges and latched closure, recalled to her the difficulty
of quietly opening the thing late at night, and of the frequency
with which her mother would then appear even when Annabeth
thought she had succeeded in so doing. It occurred to her—
seeing her mother bending to get out two bottles of beer almost as
soon as she'd removed her coat—that the sound of the refrigerator opening had not been the cause of those visits, after all.
Maybe her mother had just wanted an excuse to sit with the only
other female on the premises when the house was quiet, when
the chores were done. Annabeth took the beer from her mother's
hand and tossed down a cold gulp. That took care of the aching in
her throat, anyway.

Annabeth thought nothing of the four o'clock beer. In fact, she
liked the tacit understanding that they both needed one. She'd always appreciated her mother's easygoing attitude toward alcohol.
Annabeth and Jeff had occasionally been served small amounts
of beer or wine from the time they were twelve or thirteen. (It
seemed "very European" at the time. Eva also insisted on serving

dinner at seven, while everyone else in the entire town seemed to have it at six, if not five-thirty.) Her reaction to her husband's occasional binges had been fairly sanguine too—there had been no hiding of bottles and threatening to leave. Their fights were never about Gus's drinking, only about his disappearances. In the years since he'd left them, however, Eva had taken up where Gus had left off. Not that she had any conscious sense of completing her husband's mission of dissolution—it was just that when her rage over his final departure at last gave way to loneliness, she discovered that his preferred drink, rye whiskey, almost hit the spot.

At dinner, Annabeth watched her mother put away two large tumblers of rye and soda without apparent mishap. After Eva poured her third round, Annabeth allowed herself to say, "I didn't know you liked that stuff."

Eva shrugged almost goofily. "They say menopause does things to your sense of taste," she said.

Annabeth told herself she had come home to "take refuge and regroup." This had seemed like a perfectly reasonable goal before her departure and had even held up as she sat on the airplane, halfheartedly watching the terrible movie *Car 54, Where Are You?* But after two days in Duluth, she could no longer imagine what she had meant by "refuge." It was getting cold outside; she no longer owned any truly warm clothing. She had planned to spend her time on the couch, working her way down the shelf of books that had soothed her when she was young—Dickens, Brontë, Grimm, Grahame—but she found that her mother now used the living room for watching videotapes most evenings and, stranger still, that the movies Eva was watching were the ones Annabeth had fallen in love with in film school and during her early years in Los Angeles. (She had filled her occasional letters home with observations about cinema in lieu of more problematic information about boyfriends, money, and depression.) Eva had taken her daughter's critical assessments entirely seriously, however—something Annabeth herself had never done.

"I think you're right about *Alice Doesn't Live Here Anymore*," she said at breakfast one morning later that week, apropos of nothing. "It seems like the work of a different person than *Mean Streets* or *Taxi Driver.*"

"I know," said Annabeth, dumbfounded. She knew she should have engaged in a discussion of some sort, but she didn't know how. And when she tried to pick it up again at dinner, the game had changed,

"Is it true that Jodie Foster is a lesbian?" asked Eva.

"Jesus, Mom, how should I know?"

"Well, aren't you one?"

Annabeth blinked helplessly. She was speechless, but the question seemed to demand an answer—even if the person asking it was as potted as a plant. Eva pressed her advantage: "You never mention any boyfriends."

"I don't think I've mentioned any girlfriends, either."

"So you have them." Eva said this with a defeated tone, beginning already to dramatically mourn her tragic loss of a daughter, or her unborn grandchildren, or something . . .

"Mom, I'm not a lesbian. David? You've heard me talk about David. He's my boyfriend. We've been living together for a year and a half."

"He sounds like a fag when he answers the phone," said Eva.

Annabeth didn't know where to go with that. The urge to argue was defeated by her underlying sense that calling David her boyfriend was, at best, disingenuous.

The next night, while they were playing Scrabble and Eva was taking her usual eternity to engineer a devastating, multiscoring, close-to-vowelless play, Annabeth found her gaze drifting toward Jeff's college graduation photograph, which sat on a shelf across the room and was badly in need of dusting. Still, there was no equivalent picture of Annabeth anywhere in the house.

"Jeff looks like Dad in that picture, doesn't he?"

Eva didn't look up from her tiles. "I suppose he does." She then laid DINGY across the top of LOBE and LEAK to create both GLOBE and YE, for a total of twenty-seven points.

"You're unbeatable," said Annabeth.

Eva looked up with a strangely vulnerable expression on her face. "I was beaten a long time ago," she said.

"Well, if you were, which I sincerely doubt is the whole story, it certainly isn't *my* fault."

"No . . ." Eva answered, turning the board around to face her daughter.

The complete story of Gus Jensen's disappearance had been her mother's tragic secret. *Of course we all know what really happened,* Eva used to say. But Annabeth didn't. All she knew was that one day her father left and never came back, but what day, or where he went, or why had always been unknowable and unaskable, as blank as the wild-card Scrabble tile. The secret remained a mystery, and why it was a mystery also remained a secret. It might have been funny if she could have heard herself say it but, as a feeling in the pit of her stomach, it was just bitter and sad. There was no way on earth she could spell a word into the maze her mother had laid before her.

"Remember how you used to pretend that Dad was coming home anytime?"

"I wasn't pretending."

Foiled, Annabeth waited for more from her mother. Nothing was forthcoming. Finally she decided to strike back with her own sad story: "You know, a few months ago I got fired from the best job I ever had. My big break, and I blew it."

Eva scowled, but Annabeth had her attention. "But getting fired wasn't even the fucked-up part. Because when I finally saw it—the movie I'd been cutting?—the director had added a bunch of scenes she'd stolen from me, childhood memories . . ." Annabeth waited for a reaction, but Eva just looked puzzled.

"How can someone steal your memories?"

"She used them without asking me. Isn't that stealing, in your book? I thought you'd be outraged."

"I still don't understand. Hadn't you read the script?" Annabeth's lungs felt spongy, her heart small and hard. She had expected to be accused of treachery, to be raged at and excoriated and then, ultimately, forgiven. Instead, she was being *humored* . . . She tried to refocus on her Scrabble tiles.

"What sort of 'scenes' did she use, exactly?" Eva asked.

"What difference does it make?"

"Well, I just wondered if I was in any of them."

"Well then, Mom, you can relax."

Annabeth played the rest of her tiles hastily and badly. She was as angry at Laura as she'd ever been, angrier maybe, but this time she knew that the only possible remedy was to walk away.

That night, she lay awake for a long time, listening to a blizzard. When she finally fell asleep, she dreamed that she was recutting the scene in *Cutter's Way* that she and Laura had watched together in Lone Pine. In the dream version, Annabeth herself was the drunk Maureen, but Jeff Bridges's character was played by Laura, and the smug, handsome-sounding voice of her husband, Greg, seemed to narrate as she leaned in to kiss Annabeth. Annabeth knew she was supposed to duck the kiss and reach for the bottle instead; only in the dream, she didn't. She just sat there and felt herself being kissed by the wrong mouth, the tongue meaty and smelling of whiskey. Still dreaming, Annabeth tapped the Avid keys that would stop the playback and correct the scene, but it just kept reverting to the same form. She used to frequently have dreams of this type, but this was the first of its kind where she was a player in the intractable footage in addition to being the editor whose job it was to make it cut.

In Los Angeles, it was raining. El Niño, the baby, was throwing a fit. David couldn't remember ever before being so bombarded, either with rain or with technical explanations about the trade winds and the thermocline of the eastern Pacific. The house on Nowita seemed to spring new leaks each day, each hour sometimes. At first he kept up with them, even going so far as to buy big blue buckets at Smart & Final Iris, but as the weeks wore on, he found himself retreating. Mildew had begun to blossom somewhere in the storage room, and he was allergic. He knew he should call the landlord, he knew he shouldn't continue to lie there in the gloomy bedroom with his nose stopped up, but he couldn't figure out what to do without Annabeth. Nor could he admit to himself that Annabeth was probably never coming back.

He had his own El Niño theory, having to do with the recent earthquake, global warming, and the slow drift of atmospheric residue from the incinerated oil fields in Kuwait. As he lay in bed during the many mornings when he should have been asleep, waiting for some hope or sign of Annabeth's return, or at very least a phone call, he began to imagine a rather nightmarish personification of "the baby," and to hate the thing. The baby had taken away his girlfriend, his shelter, his sunshine, and his health, and all he had left to moor him were the occasional disembodied voices that came in on the request line during the dark, eerie winter mornings. He somehow drifted to the studios and back, but lying there in bed he began to wonder who would notice or care if he didn't. His foot had finally healed, but now the injury seemed to have relocated itself inside him somewhere. He could sometimes taste it in the back of his mouth. Annabeth had called exactly twice, sounding sardonic but chatty. Her mother still considered long-distance calling a luxury, she said. She never spoke about her plans, and he never asked. Instead, they talked about the weather.

Annabeth suspected that David was exaggerating the leaks and the dampness to elicit her pity. She could hear that he was suffering, but she told herself the problem was his sinuses, and it was his own fault if he wouldn't take care of himself. She couldn't do it for him; she had never been able to. He wanted too much.

32

Eight weeks after its premiere, *Trouble Doll* had done better than Laura had feared and not nearly as well as she had hoped: good reviews, poor distribution. Her opportunities to influence either outcome had now passed—only her disastrous financial position and limping marriage to attend to . . . which was why she was at yoga, lying supine in what was supposed to have been a thought-less state: *shavasana,* corpse pose. It was cheaper than getting a massage and a facial and usually made her feel almost as good. She'd chosen the class on the basis of schedule rather than teacher, however, and had been disappointed by ninety minutes in which there had been a lot of breathing exercises and nothing that really caused her to break a sweat. It was a small group (the regulars were people who couldn't hack a "real" class, she decided) and so the teacher, a pretty, soft-spoken woman named Sarah, had been able to pay a good deal of attention to Laura: she'd pulled back her hips in downward-facing dog, repositioned her torso in triangle pose, and gently pulled and released her head just moments earlier, in final relaxation. It was that last gesture, in fact, that seemed to have awakened a train of thought about Annabeth, who had performed many such small strategic adjustments on Laura's movie. Eventually Annabeth would realize, Laura hoped, that her childhood memories had made the movie better in the same way her clever cuts and careful pacing had done. Like a strand of pearls, a movie gains luster from everyone who touches it, and Annabeth's fingerprints were all over *Trouble Doll*. Someday, she'd get over it and be proud.

The teacher issued her instruction to "very slowly and gently wiggle your fingers and toes," which meant that after another few moments of sitting and then bowing forward and chanting *Om*, the yoga class would be over. She would then have to get back in to her by now too hot Jeep (she'd had to park on the street) and make her way back to the house, and the husband, and the problem of what to do next. Greg should come to this class, she decided. It might help him get out of his funk, and it wouldn't be too difficult physically. She would even volunteer to come with him, if that would help. He would like the soft-spoken Sarah, and he certainly couldn't find himself comparing badly with the sixtyish bald guy, the crispy surfer dude, or the asexual youth in baggy homespun shorts . . . in what universe was *that* look a good look? she wondered. Now she was bowing. "*Namaste*," she murmured in a sincere-sounding whisper, wondering if "I honor the light in myself and in others" was a reliable translation and, if so, whether it was in any way true for her at that moment, or if she even wanted it to be.

She stopped for an iced latte on the way to the car and looked in the windows of a few stores on Main Street but saw nothing to her taste. When she wasn't working, there was almost nothing else to do in L.A. but shop. She had thought about taking up hiking, or gardening, or mountain biking . . . but she was perfectly happy with running, yoga, and dieting (and/or starving) and the great outdoors was never a good place to network.

33

Annabeth was alone in the living room when her brother, Jeff, showed up more or less out of nowhere one Saturday. He lived in Eden Prairie—a good four-hour drive on snowy roads. Annabeth had never liked Jeff, really, if it was possible to say that about your own brother. He was just enough older that he had always seemed foreign to her. After their father had taken off for the last time, she'd experienced a spell of looking up to him and sometimes even feeling that he was looking *out* for her but, since college, they had hardly kept in touch. Now she saw that he'd aged badly (much more than their mother seemed to have), and Annabeth could only just align the face of the Jeff she remembered with the soft-edged, bald-headed Middle American who'd parked his Saturn in the gravel driveway. He embraced her awkwardly and half-smiled, half-winced as he said, "Behold, the return of the prodigal daughter."

"Behold, yourself," said Annabeth, surprised at the instantaneous re-creation of sibling snottiness between them.

"Let's try that again," said Jeff. "Hi, Annabeth. It's nice to see you."

She looked at his eyes and found them sincere. "Hi, Jeff," she said and then, after another second, "Can I take your coat?"

"I think I remember where we keep the closet," he said. "Where's Mom?"

"Upstairs. Headache."

"Drunk?"

"I don't think so," said Annabeth, surprised by the question.

"I guess you got spared that gene," Jeff said. "You look well, is what I mean."

"Thanks," said Annabeth. "I was just . . . reading. In the kitchen. It's warmer in there."

"Okay," said Jeff, and having hung up his coat, followed his sister.

Gradually, Annabeth gathered that Jeff's unannounced visit had as much to do with *not* being where his wife, Sheryl, was as with any great longing for a family reunion, but he did seem to be genuinely interested in her life, and that felt very strange. Just as she had designed it to be, her stuttering career in Hollywood was an object of fascination from the vantage point of northern Minnesota. Jeff spent almost an hour asking her questions and listening to her answers—not interrogating her, just building up enough rapport so that, by the following afternoon, Annabeth felt almost close to him. She and her mother prepared the near equivalent of an old-fashioned Sunday supper to feed him before he set off on the drive back home the next morning.

Cooking with her mother turned out to be fun. Much more fun than Scrabble, in any case. They made roast chicken (with two lemons in the cavity, as Annabeth had learned to do from David), and scalloped potatoes, and green bean casserole (since they would not all be together on Thanksgiving), and apple pie. Annabeth found that she still knew her way around this kitchen better than any kitchen she'd had since leaving home and that the continuing existence of certain items and implements (the rolling pin with the green wooden handles, the wire basket of lemons in the refrigerator) gave her a great sense of order and equanimity. The kitchen she shared with David, she realized, was a barely contained disaster area—and had been that way well before she'd gone back to work, before the earthquake even. Chicken or no chicken, that was a bad sign.

At one point, Eva left the room and put an old Beatles record on the console in the living room: *Rubber Soul*. Pleased with the nods of approval she got from both children on this choice, she poured herself the evening's inaugural drink. She offered one to Jeff, as well, who demurred. Annabeth, she knew, would help herself to a beer if she wanted one. They all sat at the kitchen table engaged in their respective tasks (bean snapping, potato eyeing, apple skinning, coring, and slicing) until the song "Norwegian Wood" came on.

"I've never known the Norwegians to be particularly renowned for woodwork," said Eva.

" 'Danish Wood' doesn't have enough syllables," said Anna-beth. "It's funny, though, I've never noticed that before."

Eva had been ready to be irritated by her daughter's instanta-neous rejoinder but had to forestall her irritation after Annabeth's second remark. Jeff saw the whole thing but didn't say a word. When the song ended, Annabeth repeated the phrase "This bird had flown" aloud, for no particular reason.

"Thinking about heading back?" asked Eva.

"Me? No," said Annabeth. "The phrase just struck me. When I was little I thought he was saying *Whispered alone,* like he said the word *alone* to himself when he saw she was gone."

Eva rose to bring her bowl of skinned and eyed potatoes to the counter for chopping. After taking the proper knife out of the drawer, she turned to speak to Annabeth again:

"Have you told Jeff about your problem with that Jewish woman?"

"Come again?" said Jeff.

"Laura Katz. That's a Jewish name, isn't it?"

"It doesn't make her Jewish any more than Jensen makes me Lutheran," said Annabeth. Jeff snickered.

"Well, be that as it may . . ."

"So what did the Jew do to you?" said Jeff, delighted to be needling both his mother and his sister simultaneously.

"I'm not sure," said Annabeth.

"Oh, for Christ sakes," said Eva, wiping her hands on her apron. "She decided to adopt some of our dirty laundry and put it in a movie, that's what."

"God, where did she start?" said Jeff. "Uncle Albert the em-bezzler? Great-grandfather Olaf the scab?"

"Hardly," said Annabeth, "just some of my stupid memories about growing up . . . about Dad." She still felt guilty for having even mentioned her father. But why? The more she heard other people's reactions to her complaint, the more trivial it seemed.

"About Dad? What about him?" asked Jeff.

"You know," said Annabeth lamely.

"That he abandoned us," said Eva. "Abandoned you," she corrected, pouring herself another drink.

"Why not you?" asked Annabeth.

"I threw him out," replied her mother with a kind of smugness. She jiggled her ice for emphasis. "On his ass, I might add."

This statement didn't correspond with the memory of either child, but in point of fact, neither child could remember a particular time when their father had left for good. Annabeth had often wondered, in later years, why they were so sure he wasn't coming back. Once, she'd even entertained a fantasy that her mother had killed him and cut him up into parts that were buried in the backyard or stored in the root cellar. But that was what women did to husbands who beat them or terrorized them. Her father had been entirely docile and apologetic about his periods of absence. You don't need to kill someone like that to get rid of him; you just have to wait him out and change the locks. Or, she now realized, you could just tell him to get lost, which was apparently what had actually happened.

The next morning, Annabeth woke up early and hungry. Downstairs, she found her brother staring at the kitchen floor, waiting for the coffee to drip. She sat down across from him and began to free a section of the paper from the still-folded sheaf on the table.

To her surprise, Jeff reached over without looking and patted her hand. Her impulse was to pull away, and though she didn't, she could tell that Jeff had sensed it. He looked out the window at the backyard, where the McMansions now loomed. A lot of the snow had melted and the light outside was overcast and flat.

"Dad once made me promise never to leave him alone with the two of you," Jeff said.

"What?"

"I was about ten, I think."

"Back up, start over."

"I just remembered this conversation. Mom was sitting with you on a blanket out there and Dad and I were sitting here look-ing out the window. Well, I guess he was looking out the window; I was doing something else. Homework? Anyway, he said, 'Look at that,' but I couldn't figure out what I was supposed to be seeing—it was just you and Mom fooling around with some dolls. You were, what, four or five? I kept thinking there was something hid-den in the picture somewhere, like in the *Ranger Rick* maga-zines."

"I don't remember ever playing outside with Mom."

"Maybe you were three. Anyway, I went back to my homework or the comics or whatever and then the next time I looked up, Dad was crying."

"Jeez."

"Yeah. I don't remember exactly what he said then, but the gist of it was that he thought he wasn't up to being a dad and that I was getting old enough that I should be ready to help him out sometimes—whatever the hell that meant. He said being alone with you made him feel too weak."

"Ugh. Do you remember what you said?"

" 'Okay, Dad'? What was I going to say?"

Again, Annabeth saw Jeff's adult face as it was instead of the adolescent mask she tended to see—the red in his blue eyes, the gray in his formerly brown hair. "How many years did you have *that* hanging over you?"

"Yeah," he said, nodding. "But when I think about it now, what I really think about is her." He said "her" as though Eva were right there, sitting with them, instead of upstairs sleeping off the previous night's excesses. "No wonder she turned into flint."

"Flint," Annabeth repeated. He had nailed it. Who has sympathy for flint? "Have you ever told Sheryl that story?" she asked him after they had been silent for a while.

"No, I haven't."

"Why not, do you think?"

"I don't know. Why would I?"

"To make her love you more," Annabeth responded, as though this answer was obvious. But she was surprised by how wrong it sounded, when spoken aloud.

Part 6

SMART AND FINAL

34

When Annabeth returned to L.A., she moved out of the house on Nowita Court. She told David she needed to sort herself out, and he seemed to understand. At any rate, he didn't put up a fight. Then, after a month or so of house-sitting Peter's girlfriend's brother's dismally empty apartment in Santa Monica, she went to work on the first job she could find (another independent feature, referred by Janusz). She also went back to the Al-Anon meeting in Brentwood. She wasn't sure which one of her parents was the "real" alcoholic, but it now seemed apparent that one of them must have been.

She didn't say anything to anyone there at first; nor did she buy the books, repeat the slogans, or accept the hugs of people she saw. She did find that after each meeting she felt better, though. She couldn't help but judge the other attendees—the depth of their denial, their obsessive need to control and manipulate, their endless complaints of martyrdom—and she clung to the belief that her own problems were subtler, more complicated than any of theirs.

Nevertheless, after three months of fairly regular attendance, she began to raise her hand and speak and found herself full to bursting with things to say. At first, it was all about Laura: her opportunism, her perfidy, her five-hundred-dollar face cream, her husband's transparent sweatpants. But the healing thing, Annabeth began to discover as she went on talking, was to speak without trying to elicit sympathy—to describe her experience in such a way that she could actually hear her own rage and self-pity and, as Denise had always advised, "let it go." She had almost forgiven herself for treating David so badly when she learned that he had killed himself.

Annabeth drove directly to Brentwood after David's memorial service and sat for over an hour at the coffee bar in Dutton's bookstore, waiting for her meeting to begin. She wanted to go there and spill her guts, to "turn over" the weight of her guilt and remorse once and for all. But once she began to speak, she found herself instead telling the story of how much she had hated her first visit to Al-Anon, and how she had sought refuge afterward at the catering-supplies store. She told them about how badly she had then wanted to force all of her life's detours and errors into a smart, final iris—like the tiny black dot at the end of a sentence, like water flushing down the drain. And as she described this fantasy of closure, she saw how it was exactly what David had meant to do with his not-so-decorative gunshot wound. He had also thought he could force the ending. But all he had really done was turn his back on a whole sunny roomful of people who loved him enough to come out and mourn him on a perfect afternoon in jacaranda season.

"I always used to look at the world in terms of big fish swallowing smaller fish—all the little victim fish like me," Annabeth told the Brentwood group. "But lately it seems more like the sea is just full of minnows, and that's it. Like, the things I was sure were *what really matters,* and the people I thought had the power to give those things to me . . . Well, there are no victims, only volunteers, is the slogan, I guess. Can you say that about a suicide?" She looked down at her hands and found that they were making fists. "I just fucking hate him for doing it," she said, expecting to feel relief for at least admitting this. The soft eyes and gentle nods around the circle meant they had heard her, but still no tears came.

35

When, three months later, Annabeth received a note in the mail from Naomi Bronstein, she was afraid to open it. It had been forwarded from the old house on Nowita—David's last address—which was in itself so gruesome that she wished she could just burn the thing. If she had written them a condolence note, or even signed the guest book at the damn memorial, they could have found her. But she had been too much of a jerk to do either. She opened the envelope, fully expecting to be torn a new asshole in the most gracious and generous of terms. Instead, she found that it contained a note card on which was written the following: "Please come have dinner with us sometime soon. Any day that suits you. We look forward to it."

Still prepared for their rage, Annabeth forced herself to punch the digits of their number into her phone. Jerry answered. "Oh, Annabeth, good!" he said. "We'd almost given up on you." He said this without apparent malice.

She had intended to apologize for not writing to them but forgot this plan entirely when Jerry suggested that she come that Sunday. "Early enough to see if there's anything here you want to keep for yourself," he said, and they agreed on five P.M. All she could think of were the flip-flops—she would rather have eaten them than looked at them ever again.

The Bronsteins lived in Mandeville Canyon, in a house that exemplified one particularly bohemian view of the late-1970s southern California lifestyle. Annabeth had never driven there before and was afraid she'd gotten hopelessly lost among the switchbacks when she recognized the ceiling lamp that David used to call "the monkey puzzle lamp." It was visible through a glass cutout in the redwood façade of the Bronsteins' home.

Naomi hugged her at the door. She was shorter than Annabeth, and also skinnier, but the skin of her face and neck was soft and smelled of some French perfume no one much wore anymore. The hug felt authentically warm and forgiving to Annabeth. She did her best to hug back.

Jerry was in the living room, working his way through an assortment of newspapers, but stood to shake Annabeth's hand. "Can I get you a drink? A glass of wine?" he asked. Annabeth knew the Bronsteins were not really drinkers but that they used to keep some beer around for David.

"I bet you have some Anchor Steam on hand," she said and then regretted it, but no one seemed particularly spooked.

Naomi got two bottles out of the refrigerator while Annabeth and Jerry smiled shyly at each other. He gestured at his pile of Sunday papers and said, "Can't find anything new in any of them. What about you?"

"No, not really," said Annabeth and took the open bottle of beer Naomi handed her while Jerry accepted the other. His wife then looked at him and said:

"Now?"

"Might as well get it over with," said Jerry.

Annabeth wondered what they had in mind for her. She couldn't bear any more guilt.

"How's Linda?" she said, meaning, Look at the bright side: you've still got a daughter. Maybe she'll give you Jewish grandchildren.

"Wonderful," said Naomi. "They're in Rome for the year. She got a residency."

Gripping the beer bottle, Annabeth followed David's mother up the banisterless wooden stairs and, for the first time in her life, consciously prayed for serenity, courage, and wisdom. David's bedroom was on the third floor, the only place in the house that got any real sunlight, and though small, it felt spacious because it had a skylight and the desk and bureau were built in. There was nothing to sit on except the bed, and no sign of the cache of belongings Annabeth had expected to have to sort through.

"We thought you might like some privacy," said Naomi. "Please, sit."

Annabeth carefully lowered herself onto the edge of the neatly made bed, its worn blue bedspread obviously a relic from David's childhood.

Naomi took an envelope from the windowsill and handed it to Annabeth. It was unsealed and bore no address but contained a sheet of folded paper that she did not need to be told had been written by David.

"We couldn't help reading it," said Naomi. "I hope you understand." She almost succeeded in saying these words without betraying her grief.

The date on the letter was ten days before David's death. They had spoken on the phone sometime that week and he had not sounded then like someone about to kill himself. This gave her the courage to read on. The letter said:

Dear Annabeth,

Happy anniversary. You don't remember the date but it was my first tryout at KCRW. I will never forget how the sun looked on your back that afternoon. I want to tell you that I am grateful for everything, because you never pretended with me. You were real. I can't say this kind of thing on the phone, it sounds pathetic, but I still love you and I don't want to hurt you though I know I'm going to.

Laura said you are not an artist but what does she know? The artists are the ones who stay at it, who keep going. Please keep going. Please forgive me.

Love, David

Naomi had left the room. Annabeth finally began to weep.

36

She woke up sweating the next morning. Overnight, the Santa Anas had blown in, the inverted hot winds that suck the moisture from eyeballs, nostrils, flowers, and lawns on their way out to sea instead of in from it. Her new apartment, a bungalow with glass doorknobs and built-in bookshelves, was at the top of a courtyard in Los Feliz—it was much warmer than the west side of town, even when the weather was pleasant. Annabeth had no air conditioner, and she'd found that her beautiful sunny rooms were rapidly becoming unbearable. In the shower, she looked at the mermaid etched into the glass door panel and decided she would drive to the beach. La Piedra: David had always talked about taking her there, but they had never gone.

It was a long drive, practically to the Ventura County line, but when she finally got to the trailhead and looked down the steep incline at the rocky beach, she felt her chest relax for the first time in weeks, or maybe longer.

She'd only swum in the Pacific twice before, both times in Malibu with groups of drunk or stoned partygoers. Alone, at midday, on the mostly deserted beach, she found the prospect of immersion both frightening and appealing. There was no lifeguard present, but the sea looked calm. Her fear was not of bodily harm so much as of the extreme solitude of leaving dry land with no one on shore to wave back to. Nevertheless, she waded in. First to hip depth, then up to her chest, and finally she took a half dozen long strokes out past the shore break. When she surfaced and looked back, she couldn't locate her white towel and black knapsack anywhere on the shore. Then she realized they were there, just much smaller than she'd expected. The current had been at her back. The water was cold but felt bouyant and tonic, and she dove under again just to feel its magic coolness on her scalp. Then she turned faceup and kicked for a while, traveling parallel to the beach. The sky was dense above her, a grayish-white screen on which she could project anything she wanted to. But she didn't want to project; she just wanted to sway there in the water, dangling, suspended. Something would come.

What came was company. She suddenly had the unmistakable sense that she was being watched and began to look for her observer—first toward shore and then out to the horizon, where she saw it. Some ten feet off, a sea lion was gazing at her with equanimity. The creature's round forehead and bright brown eyes were candid and familiar. Almost human, Annabeth thought, feeling a welling up of love for the creature. But the sea lion had seen enough. It slipped underwater and vanished, leaving a gleaming wake that Annabeth followed hungrily with her eyes.

Acknowledgments

The people in this story are fictional but their knowledge is not. Any technical skills displayed by Annabeth and Laura come from one of three sources: Walter Murch's *In the Blink of an Eye,* Michael Ondaatje's *The Conversations,* or Barbara Tulliver's cutting room, where she was kind enough to let me look over her shoulder for a few days.

Brave Dan Menaker read so many versions of this story he can probably recite portions of it in his sleep, and I thank him for all his hard work on my behalf. Dan's was a tough act to follow, but I was lucky to find Laura Ford, who has been wonderful in the crucial, final rounds of turning pages into book. Also at Random House, I have been helped and humored by Stephanie Higgs, Bonnie Thompson, and especially Evan Camfield, who seems to go above and beyond as a matter of course.

Meanwhile, in Brooklyn, Nina Collins has offered endless advice and support from the very beginning—more great luck on my part. And for making Nina's trains run on time, I thank Matthew Elblonk, who does everything right, always, and with a sense of humor.

Other generous readers, near and far: Julie Applebaum, Lori Bongiorno, Sheila Colon, Gail Fath, Kara Lindstrom, Naomi Rand, Julia Schacter, Jane South, and Jenny Snider. No one has helped more, or more gracefully, perceptively, and thoroughly, however, than Joe Gioia, the smartest guy I know and the most unafraid of commas.

Which leaves only Patty Wolff, who coined the epithet "my liar" and lived to tell the tale. I'm relieved to say that I have appropriated it for use in this book with her permission.

ABOUT THE AUTHOR

A native and current resident of Brooklyn, New York,
RACHEL CLINE lived in Los Angeles from 1990 to
1999. During that time she wrote screenplays and
teleplays, designed interactive media, and taught
screenwriting at USC. Her first novel, *What to Keep*,
was published in 2004.

www.rachelcline.com

ABOUT THE TYPE

This book was set in Fairfield, the first typeface from the hand of the distinguished American artist and engraver Rudolph Ruzicka (1883–1978). Ruzicka was born in Bohemia and came to America in 1894. He set up his own shop, devoted to wood engraving and printing, in New York in 1913 after a varied career working as a wood engraver, in photoengraving and banknote printing plants, and as an art director and freelance artist. He designed and illustrated many books, and was the creator of a considerable list of individual prints—wood engravings, line engravings on copper, and aquatints.